KING CANYON HIDEOUT

Levi Hill, Pinkerton range detective, huddles in his saddle against the fierce thunderstorm. Is he riding into an ambush? Men have been killed in cold blood, and even now, as Levi follows the stolen cattle through the rain, he senses that hidden eyes are following him. Suddenly the crash of a rifle rings out above the fury of the storm. With death surrounding him, Lord only knows if his skills with guile and gun can finally bring peace to the range.

BILLY HALL

KING CANYON HIDEOUT

Complete and Unabridged

LINFORD
Leicester

First published in Great Britain in 1998 by
Robert Hale Limited
London

First Linford Edition
published 1999
by arrangement with
Robert Hale Limited
London

The right of Billy Hall to be identified as
the author of this work has been asserted by
him in accordance with the
Copyright, Designs and Patents Act, 1988

British Library CIP Data

Hall, Billy
    King Canyon hideout.—Large print ed.—
    Linford western library
    1. Western stories
    2. Large type books
    I. Title
    823.9'14 [F]

    ISBN 0–7089–5518–5

Published by
F. A. Thorpe (Publishing) Ltd.
Anstey, Leicestershire

Set by Words & Graphics Ltd.
Anstey, Leicestershire
Printed and bound in Great Britain by
T. J. International Ltd., Padstow, Cornwall

This book is printed on acid-free paper

1

Dust swirled in the lazy heat of the late afternoon. It hung in the air, as though reluctant to lie again on the hot dry earth. The horses shared the dust's lack of any will to hurry, content merely to drift where they were driven.

Sure too hot'n dry for the front end o' March, Robert thought. Oughta be cold and blustery, this far north.

He slowed his mount, letting the driven horses ease on ahead. They were well broken to the trail, and no trouble. As the last of the thirty-three head moved past, his brother caught up. 'You ready to eat this dust a while?'

'Hey, I rode drag all day yesterday,' Robert drawled in return. ' 'Sides, I reckon a little dirt'll be good fer ye. Take some o' that sass outa ya.'

The elder brother pulled his neckerchief down from its shielding of his

1

nose and mouth, and grinned. 'What sass?' he asked in mock innocence. 'What are you talkin' about?'

'You know what I'm talkin' about. You was lookin' purty sassy with that little ol' gal back there on Pepper Crick.'

'Aw, c'mon! She was sweet on me! I cain't help it if the girls like me.'

'Yeah, you looked real sorrowful 'bout it.'

'She was kinda purty, wasn't she?' Ralph reflected.

'I ain't sure we oughta keep goin' north,' Robert changed the subject abruptly.

'Why not? Hey, we're doin' good, Robert. We done started out with eight head when we crossed the Cimarron. Now we got us thirty-three head, and nigh on to fifty dollars to boot. They's a real need for well-broke horses in this country.'

'Yeah, but it's gettin' too hot 'n dry,' Robert complained. 'This here's kinda farm country, too. If they don't get some rain purty quick, they won't be buyin' nothin'. They'll all just be wantin' to sell us what horses they already got, just fer cash.'

'It's sure hot, all right,' Ralph agreed. 'Hey, there goes that danged roan again. I'm ridin' drag. You gotta catch 'im!'

Robert had already seen the big roan stud veer off from the bunch and start trotting off on his own course. A couple of the mares were following his lead. Robert jabbed his horse lightly with his spurs and leaned forward and yelled, 'Heeaah, boy. Let's go get him!'

His horse responded instantly. His ears lay back flat against his head. He lunged forward and stretched out with his belly almost brushing the grass. In four jumps he had reached full stride. He ran with abandon, running flat out across the already dry grass of the Nebraska prairie.

Robert grinned against the wind in his face. The front of his hat brim blew up flat against its high crown.

He leaned forward until his face was just above the outstretched neck of his mount. The hot air felt cooler as it whistled past his ears. The ground beneath them turned to a blur.

The big roan stud broke into a run, determined to keep to the course he had set for himself. He was no match for the speed of the buckskin gelding Robert was riding, though. The distance between them closed rapidly.

The stallion saw he had no chance to outrun the other, so abruptly he began to turn back in the direction of the herd. As Robert circled him, the great gelding swung in close to the other horse. Robert shook out a couple coils of his lariat as they ran. He used it as a whip, lashing the rump of the rebellious stallion, hastening his return.

By the time he and the mares who had started to follow him were returned to the shambling bunch, Robert's horse was streaked with sweat.

'Dang it, Robert!' Ralph yelled at

him, as the younger brother returned to his side. 'What are you tryin' to do? You didn't have to catch 'im afore he got a hunnert yards off! It's too hot to be runnin' your horse that way.'

'Wow! Cain't this ol' boy run?' Robert exulted.

'You'll think he can run, when he sticks his foot in a badger hole, an' busts 'is leg!' Ralph continued to fuss.

As if in answer, Robert's horse snorted and tossed his head, eager to run some more. 'I bet in a quartermile this here horse could just about beat anything in the country,' he bragged.

Ralph only grunted, spitting dust and wiping his mouth with the back of his hand. He pulled his neckerchief back up over his nose and mouth.

Suddenly a jack-rabbit lunged from almost beneath his horse's feet. He ran to Robert's right in long, leaping strides, ears and tail flashing tall in the air. A large .45 appeared as if by magic in Robert's hand and roared. The jack-rabbit leaped high in the air, somersaulting backward. Landing in the tall, dry grass he thrashed violently for half a minute, then lay still.

At the roar of the shot, the entire bunch of horses shied violently and ran several steps, then stopped and looked in the direction from which it came. Ralph ripped the neckerchief from his face again. 'Dang you, Robert!' he yelled in exasperation. 'You tryin' to spook the whole bunch?'

'Bet I got 'im right in the eye,' Robert yelled back, grinning. 'What d'ya bet?'

He nudged his horse and trotted over to where the rabbit lay. Jumping from his horse he picked it up. 'Tol' you so! Right in the eye!'

Ralph shook his head in exasperation. He jerked the neckerchief back up over his face and kept the bunch moving. Robert quickly cleaned and skinned the rabbit. He took off his own neckerchief, and shook the dust out of it. From his canteen he wet it thoroughly.

He tied the rabbit to a saddle string, then covered it with the wet neckerchief. 'That'll keep you wet 'n cool till supper-time, ol' feller,' he told the dead rabbit.

Mounting his horse, he set out at a fast trot to catch up with his brother and the retreating bunch of horses.

'We musta covered pert near ten miles today,' Ralph greeted him, as he caught up. ' 'Bout time to find a place to water the horses and camp for the night.'

'I seen a wisp o' smoke comin' outa this next draw while ago,' Robert responded. 'I reckon they's a place there. They'll likely let us water 'em.'

Within the hour, they came to the ranch buildings nestled just over the top of a large hill. To the south and west, the site was protected from the winter winds by the hill. To the east and north, the view stretched unimpeded.

'Nice home site,' Ralph observed.

Robert nodded silently. His eyes

were busy taking in all the features of the house, the barn, the corrals. A large windmill dominated the yard. It pumped into a huge, tall supply tank. From the supply tank pipes ran to a water tank in each of the corrals. Several pieces of farm machinery and haying equipment were lined up neatly behind the barn.

'They even got some saw-milled boards,' he said. 'Right prosperous place. I betcha we can sell that pair of percherons here.'

'Got real machinery all right,' Ralph agreed. 'Might not have any money, though. What we askin'?'

'Fifty dollars,' Robert replied without hesitation.

'What we takin'?' the elder brother asked.

'Forty, maybe,' he grinned, then turned suddenly serious. 'No less'n that. They's a good pair.'

A tall, lanky man came into sight walking across the yard. He stopped when he saw the bunch of horses coming. Putting his hand up, he shielded his eyes and watched for several minutes. He turned and walked to the biggest of the corrals. He opened the gate wide in an invitation that could not be mistaken, then walked across the yard to a place that would not hinder the horses' entry. The horses, already smelling the water in the tanks, quickened their steps. As though they had been there all their lives, the two huge percherons trotted directly to the open gate. As they entered they wheeled to the left, looking like they were yoked together and marching in step. They trotted directly to the tank, burying their dusty muzzles in the cool liquid in perfect unison.

The rest of the horses followed, except for the three young mustangs. The two pintos and one bay, stopped, snorting at the unfamiliar trappings of the yard and corral. Ralph and Robert moved up behind them. Robert spoke softly to them.

'Moop, moop, moop,' he crooned a soothing nonword. 'Get on in there. Moop, moop. C'mon boys, move on in.'

The horses tossed their heads, pawing the ground nervously. Finally the bay trotted through the gate, shying at it as he passed, then running across the corral before returning to the tank to drink. The other two broke into a run, galloping through the gate and into the corral.

The dusty, sweat-streaked pair swung off their horses. Ralph stepped to the corral, closing the gate, while Robert went the other way, to greet the rancher as he approached. He held out his hand. 'Howdy,' he greeted. 'Thanks for the welcome. The horses was gettin' just a tad dry.'

'Well, put up your own horses too and come on in the house,' the stranger said, returning Robert's firm grip. 'Ma'll have some supper cooking before long. You boys will stay and eat a bite, won't you?'

'Well, thank you. That's mighty nice of you. We'll let the horses drink, then we'll turn 'em out and let 'em graze, if that's all right. Then we'll just be plumb happy to eat with you.'

The man nodded. 'They look like well-cared for horses,' he approved.

'Yeah, they're 'most all real fine horses,' Robert said, sounding suddenly like a horse trader. 'Real fine horses. Say, I shot a rabbit while ago. Do you reckon you folks could use it?'

'Sure, we'd use it.'

'I cleaned 'im right away,' Robert explained. 'Put my neckerchief on 'im to keep 'im from dryin' out. I'll wash 'im off in the tank, then bring 'im to the house while the horses is drinkin'.'

He and Ralph led their horses to the side of the tank that stuck through the outside of the corral. They pulled off the bridles, then put them back on with the bits hanging below their mouths. That allowed the horses to drink without the bits bothering, but left the bridles in place so they could be tethered with the reins.

Robert rinsed out his neckerchief in the tank. He wrung it as dry as possible and put it back around his neck. He washed the rabbit thoroughly, then washed his hands and face in the tank. When his hands were clean he cupped them below the pipe coming from the supply tank. Catching the clean fresh water, he lifted his hands to his mouth quickly, savouring the cool refreshing liquid.

'Good water,' he commented.

'No alkali at all,' Ralph agreed, doing the same.

The rancher had returned, so Robert handed him the rabbit. He took it wordlessly. Robert watched with amusement as he turned the rabbit over twice, looking for bullet holes. Seeing none, he knew it was head-shot. He gave an almost imperceptible nod of approval.

When the horses were turned loose to graze, the two returned to the house. In response to their knock, a large, raw-boned woman opened the door. 'Come in, boys,' she said. 'Oh, I see you washed up already. Just go on in and sit down. Supper's almost ready.'

2

The shade of the house was a welcome contrast to the heat. Ralph and Robert took off their hats as they entered. The rancher's wife noted their guns and frowned noticeably. Without waiting for an introduction, she said, 'I would appreciate it if you wouldn't wear your guns in the house.'

Ralph began to unbuckle his gunbelt at once, but Robert hesitated. Finally he did so as well, untying the thong that held the bottom of the holster firmly to his leg, then removing the belt and holster. Fastening the buckles again, they hung them on pegs just inside the door and went on in to the dining-room. A young woman was just finishing setting the table. As she turned, both boys caught their breath sharply.

She smiled; a great, relaxed, smile

that bore no hint of self-consciousness. 'Hi!' she said brightly. 'I'm Mattie.'

Ralph returned the smile. 'I'm Ralph Blundell,' he said, putting the accent on the second syllable of the name. 'This here's my little brother, Robert. Mattie, you said your name is? That's a pretty name. Like you.'

She started to respond, but her father chose that moment to walk in from the interior of the house. 'Well boys,' he said, 'you get the horses taken care of?'

They both nodded, and Robert spoke. 'We just turned 'em out to graze. They're tired. They won't wander off. Grass is dry, but it's good grass. Last year musta been a sight wetter'n this year.'

Their host nodded. 'Oh, I'm sorry. I guess I'm forgettin' my manners. My name's Henry Hawkinson. This here's my wife, Esther, and my daughter, Matilda.'

'Father,' the girl remonstrated. 'You know I don't like that name!' She

15

smiled at Robert. 'Please, just call me Mattie. Matilda sounds so terribly old-fashioned.'

Henry looked like he was about to say something, but he chose to introduce the rest of the people at the long table instead. 'And these are our two hands, Hans DeVeer and Homer Overocker.'

'I'm Robert Blundell,' Robert responded, putting that same accent on the last syllable. 'This is my brother, Ralph. We sure thank you for your hospitality.'

'Vel, by golly, you don't look like you ist from around dis country,' Hans offered. 'Haf you boys come far?'

They both nodded, but Ralph spoke. 'West Texas. We're from about two days' south of the Cimarron.'

'I thought your accent sounded like Texas,' Esther Hawkinson said, carrying in a huge platter of steaming meat. 'You boys are awfully young to be that far from home, aren't you?'

The corners of Ralph's mouth

tightened, but he said nothing. Robert reddened slightly. 'No ma'am,' he disagreed. 'Me'n Ralph, we been on our own quite a spell. We been tradin' horses 'round the country fer nigh on four years a'ready.'

'Really?' she responded. 'You don't look that old. How old are you?'

'Now, Ma,' Henry remonstrated. 'Don't go pryin'.'

'I'm not prying,' she argued. 'Just asking. How old did you boys say you were?'

They both cleared their throats. 'I'm seventeen a'ready,' Robert said. 'Ralph, he's pert near nineteen.'

'You've been on your own since you were thirteen?' she asked aghast. 'Why, that's awful! I . . . '

'Been horse tradin' all that time?' Henry interjected, interrupting his wife.

Robert eagerly grasped at the change of subject. 'Yes sir. We done took a string o' horses up through Colorado, last year.'

'Colorado, huh?'

'Yup. Done went up to Cripple Crick an' Leadville, an' all them mountain places.'

'Pretty tough country, I hear,' Henry mused.

'Aw, we don't mind,' Ralph bragged. 'We can hold our own.'

'I, uh, see a pretty good-looking pair of work horses in your string,' Henry offered. 'They come from around here?'

'Kansas,' Robert replied immediately. 'Can't remember the feller's name we got 'em off. Got it on his bill o' sale, though.'

Henry nodded. 'Why did he trade them off?' he asked, making a rather transparent effort to sound casual.

'Just plumb went busted. Quit farmin'. Dried out. He was fixin' to head out West and didn't have no use fer two teams. Had 'im a fine team o' Clydesdales we tried to trade 'im outa, but he wanted them to pull his wagon. We thought the percherons'd be better'n steadier, but he liked the way them Clydesdales stepped. They sure are showy, all right.'

'Buy 'em for cash, did you?'

'Naw, we done traded 'im a real good pair o' saddle horses. Now, if you was needin' a team for farmin', I reckon that pair would make you as fine a team as you could get. They's gentle enough the womenfolk could work 'em. They don't kick when you harness 'em or hitch 'em up or nothin'. They ain't a bit snaky at all.'

They discussed them and other horses throughout supper, much to the obvious disappointment of both Esther and Mattie. In the end, Henry agreed to hitch the pair up the next day and try them out. No price was mentioned.

'If you want, you'd just as well corral the horses again for the night,' Henry said, as they finished supper. 'You boys are welcome to sleep in the hay mow, if you want a roof over your head.'

'Why, we'd be plumb happy to do

that,' Ralph agreed at once. 'Wouldn't we, Robert?'

As Robert was about to answer, Henry spoke again. 'There should be quite a few of the other ranchers and farmers riding in pretty shortly. We're having a meeting of the Pine Ridge Cattlemen's Association here tonight. You might even be able to do a little trading with some of them.'

Robert raised his eyebrows slightly. 'Special meetin'?'

Henry was thoughtful for a moment before he answered. 'We been having a problem with rustling in the area,' he said finally. 'Hasn't been a problem out this way much yet, but the Cattlemen's Association seems to think it's spreading out wider all the time. Anyway, I've been a member for several years. They asked to meet with a bunch of us out here in Antelope Valley. We do almost as much farming as ranching out here, but we all run some stock, too.'

At the door, both Ralph and Robert

buckled their guns on again. They walked into the yard, visiting idly with their host. He walked with them to where their saddled horses were grazing. Their front feet were hobbled together to ensure they could catch them easily, but they had managed to walk quite a ways as they grazed.

They had walked about fifty yards from the house when a dry rattling buzz froze them in their tracks. It took Robert a minute to spot the prairie rattler's head amongst the tall dry grass. He was coiled with his head raised. His tongue flicked in and out of his mouth constantly. His tail extended straight up from the centre of the coil. It was shaking rapidly, causing the rattles at its end to emit their characteristic warning.

Robert acted without thought as soon as he spotted the menace to man and animal. His hand swept out his .45 and fired in one smooth motion. The rattler's head disappeared. The headless body began a random writhing in the mindless contortions of sudden death. Henry Hawkinson's eyebrows shot up.

'Awfully handy with that gun for a young fellow,' he commented.

'My uncle taught me,' the young man responded, with no conscious effort at being brash. 'I reckon I kin hold my own with most.'

The rancher looked like he was about to say something further, but did not. He walked to the writhing body of the snake. Stepping on the headless reptile, he took his pocket knife and cut off the rattles. He dropped them in his pocket.

'Got me a collection of rattles from 'em,' he explained.

Robert and Ralph retrieved their horses, replaced the bridles, tightened the cinches, then began the relatively easy task of rounding up the remuda and hazing them back to the corral. They were still tired and hot. They offered no resistance to being returned to the ample supply of cold water the corral held.

3

'Looks like we got trouble,' Robert drawled softly.

Ralph casually turned around, resting the back of his shoulders against the corral fence. 'Does at that, little brother.'

'You know him?'

'Ain't never seen 'im afore.'

Ralph and Robert had worked like a well-practised team, retrieving their horses. By the time they had them gathered and corralled, several saddled horses were tied up in the yard. Within the next hour the number of men there grew to more than twenty. They gathered in small groups, visiting. At least half of them leaned against the corral fence, talking and studying the horses. Robert and Ralph lounged carelessly by the gate, waiting for nibbles of interest they could barter into trades.

They came to attention as one of the visiting ranchers walked purposely toward them. His forehead was furrowed in a scowl. His head was thrust forward, making it appear like he was leaning forward as he walked. Dust flew outward from his boots at each step. A second man strode with him, his square-jawed scowl matching the other man's. 'His kid or his hand?' Robert asked softly.

'Hard to say,' Ralph replied just as softly. 'Looks like he's got a burr under his saddle, though.'

The rancher standing closest to them, studying their horses, overheard the exchange. He looked over his shoulder, then turned back. 'Oscar Olson,' he offered softly. 'That's his foreman with him. Hans Lubson. Ranches along Bordeaux Crick. They're a pair o' bulls. Watch yourselves.'

He looked like he was about to say more, but the approaching pair were too close. He turned slowly and watched, worrying a wooden match from one side of his mouth to the other.

'You the ones got them horses?' Olson asked bluntly.

'Sure thing,' Robert drawled, smiling easily. 'Which one can I sell you? Got a good roan stallion that'd carry you all day.'

The big rancher did not return the smile or acknowledge the offer to trade. 'Do you have bills-of-sale for them?'

Robert's smile broadened, but his eyes showed no mirth as he responded. 'Why, sure! Never buy or sell a horse without one. Which one you interested in?'

'I'm not interested in any of them,' was the quick reply. 'I'm interested in seeing those bills-o'-sale.'

'Well, you decide you want to buy one, I'll be plumb happy to show that to you,' Robert drawled, still smiling. He stopped leaning against the corral and moved a step away from it.

'You'll show them all to me right now,' the rancher corrected. 'You come into this country with a string of horses you may or may not have title to, I want to see the bill-o'-sale.'

Robert and Ralph both moved now, putting a little distance between them. Their hands had moved to within inches of their gun butts. Robert was doing the talking and he never stopped smiling.

'Why, no, I guess I won't be doing anything of the sort. I don't know who you think you are, but as long as you ain't wearin' no badge I ain't got to show you nothin'. Tell me, do you always go around huffin' like a bull that's got so old he can't do nothin' but puff'n beller?'

The rancher's face went crimson. His foreman stepped forward and his fist started up when he noticed Robert's hand next to his gun.

'He's packin' a gun, Hans,' somebody along the corral said. 'Better watch it.'

Hans' chin jutted forward belligerently. 'You talk real big when you're facing an unarmed man, Texas boy,' the ranch foreman grated. 'Take that gun off and I'll teach you to speak to your betters with respect.'

Robert looked the huge blond up and down, satisfying himself he had no hidden weapon. With his smile still frozen on his face he replied, 'Why, I just can't think of anything I'd enjoy any more than that. I ain't had to teach nobody not to call me a boy for quite a while.'

As he spoke he untied the thong that held his holster down. He unfastened the belt buckle and swung the gun and holster from his hip. He hung it on the top of a corral post beside Ralph. 'Big brother, you see to it that nobody thinks he oughta offer this big dumb Swede any help, would you?'

As he stepped away from the gun the foreman came at him with a rush. Robert sidestepped. He arced a crushing right hook into the side of the big man's head as he went by. It felt like he'd just hit the side of a barn. It barely fazed the man.

The big man wheeled and lunged a second time. Robert stepped the other direction, hitting him in the nose with his right fist, then on the ear with a hard left as he again went by. Blood flew from his nose, but he appeared not to notice. Like a bull he wheeled and threw another lunging haymaker at Robert's elusive grin.

Again Robert sidestepped, hammering the big man as he lunged past. Robert continued to feint and dodge, smashing a continuous barrage of blows into the big man's face. It seemed to make no difference to the unrelenting attack of the foreman who had yet to lay a hand on the young Texan. He bore in, time after time, as though wanting to wear down Robert's fists with the brutality of his face.

Robert obliged the wish. He swung with the power of well-developed strength and skill. The big man's shirt was coated with blood halfway down. Blood was splattered all over

Robert as well, but it was all the other man's. Never fought nobody this long without at least gettin' hit once in a while, he thought.

The big man's face quickly turned to a mass of bruised, chopped and bleeding flesh, but his pace never slowed. Like a great mindless bull he kept boring in, grunting in pain and frustration, but giving no other sign he even felt the punishment his face and head were taking. Robert's hands began to swell and bleed. His arms ached. That fella's right, he told himself silently. This guy's a bull. He ain't got no brains, but he's a bull. What do I have to do to stop him?

He knew he had to try something different. He had chopped the man's face to ribbons and it seemed to have no effect. His own breathing had grown ragged. His feet were moving slower. The big man's last charge had been a little faster than the previous ones and he almost didn't sidestep quickly enough. He simply could not continue much longer.

The assembled men had formed a large circle. They watched without expression for the most part. It had become apparent at once that nobody intended to intervene. Ralph kept his attention on the big fighter's boss, just in case, but inwardly he relaxed and watched his brother's mastery at work.

With a gun or his fists, that boy's a wonder, he admired silently.

The foreman wiped the blood from his eyes to see his tormentor and lunged forward again. This time, instead of trying to avoid the charge, Robert stepped forward to meet it. Bringing all the strength he had, he brought an overhand right, lunging with all the power of his long legs. His fist connected with the big man's chin with the sound of a fence post hitting a tree trunk. Shock and pain radiated from Robert's hand all the way through his arm and shoulder.

The sheer force of the blow stopped

the big man in his tracks. Robert stepped back to throw a matching blow with his left, but saw the big man's eyes lose their focus. He held the punch and took a step backward.

Olson's right-hand man stood without moving for three heartbeats. His eyes glazed over. Without changing expression he leaned forward and kept leaning. Unbending, he struck the ground of the farmyard and lay without moving. Robert watched for a moment to be sure he wasn't going to move. With the smile still frozen on his face, Robert's eyes sought out the man's boss. His smile broadened a trace as he addressed the livid rancher. 'You want to take a try yourself now or do you just let your pet bull do all your fightin' fer ya?'

The man glared back into Robert's taunting smile, but said nothing. It was Robert who spoke again. 'You sure you ain't interested in one of them horses? 'Course, if your foreman's the best man you got, I ain't sure anyone on your outfit's man enough to ride any o' my horses.'

The surly rancher clenched and unclenched his fists. His crimson face appeared ready to explode. He wheeled and stalked off. Stamping his way to the horse tank he removed his neckerchief and soaked it. Returning to his foreman, he rolled him over on his back and began trying to clean the blood and dirt from his face.

Robert turned his attention to the rest. His eyes slowly went around the circle of faces. 'Anyone else wanta call me'n Ralph horse-thieves?' he drawled softly.

There was a general stirring of discomfort among the assembled ranchers. The one who had been standing closest to Ralph finally responded.

'Young man, I think we owe you an apology. Oscar means well, but he's pretty upset by all this rustling. I'm Chet Buchanan. You handle yourself pretty well!'

He stepped forward and extended a hand to Robert. He took it after only an instant's hesitation. He tried not to wince as the lanky rancher gripped its new bruises. The man shook hands with Ralph as well. 'I hope you understand, this country's generally a lot more hospitable than this,' he apologized again.

The rest of the group gathered around and introduced themselves. It was Henry Hawkinson who finally returned to the subject of the bills-of-sale.

'You know, I sure wouldn't want you fellows to take this the wrong way, but, well, there has been a lot of things going on around this country lately. I wonder if maybe, just as a favour to me, you could see fit to show these men those bills-o'-sale?'

Robert and Ralph looked at each other. The rancher continued hurriedly. 'I ain't questioning at all that you got 'em. You boys ain't got the look o' horse-thieves. The thing is, Oscar went and raised the issue. Unless we check it out, he's gonna go spreadin' all over the country that I'm harbourin' horse-thieves or somethin'.'

Ralph shrugged. Robert walked to his saddle, hung on the top of the corral fence. Reaching into one of the saddle-bags, he drew out a sheaf of papers. He handed them to Hawkinson. Several of the others gathered around Henry as he leafed through them.

'There's that Appaloosa with the Rocking-R brand,' one of them said. 'That's sure Dave Ricker's signature, all right. I bought some cows off'n him a year ago, down on Pepper Crick.'

They leafed through the papers for a minute or two longer. Hawkinson handed them back. 'Looks as straight as anything I ever seen,' he said. 'Thank you boys.' He looked around the assembled faces. 'Anybody here that ain't completely satisfied?'

Nobody offered anything but affirmative comments. 'OK then, let's get down to the business that brought you all here.

If any of you want to do some horse trading with these fellows, we'll ask them to hang around a day or two.'

They moved off toward the large front porch of the house, ignoring Olson and his still unconscious foreman. One man paused as he walked by them.

'Your man OK, Oscar?' he asked.

'He'll live,' the surly rancher growled.

The man shrugged and walked on. Ralph and Robert drifted off to the barn. Climbing to the hay mow they fixed a place on the piled hay to roll out their bedrolls and prepared to enjoy a soft night's sleep.

4

Robert tossed and turned. Ralph was snoring softly. Robert studied his hands in the soft light the moon spilled into the hay mow. They were swelling and hurt severely. He finally stood up silently and made his way back down the ladder. Moving to the water tank, he buried his hands in its cool, soothing water.

The shock of the cold water passed almost instantly and was replaced with a welcome sensation of relief. He noted absently that the man he had beaten and his boss were both gone. Musta come to, he mused silently. I doubt Olson's man enough to carry him off all by hisself.

A steady drone of voices came from the front porch of the house. Ranchers were sitting on what chairs were available, the porch railing, the steps and the yard. His curiosity finally got the better of him and he wandered over.

The first one he noticed was Oscar Olson. His mood remained unchanged. He appeared to feel compelled to argue with anything that was advanced. His battered foreman sat on the ground beside him. His head hung forward. Blood still oozed from several places on his face. He swiped dazedly at them occasionally with a bloody neckerchief he held in his hand.

Robert wandered up in full sight of all of them and leaned against a post holding the porch roof. His hands were throbbing again, but he ignored them.

Discussion was centering around the things that had been done to try to discover who was behind the rustling. It was quickly evident they didn't know who was doing it, where the cattle were being taken, how they were being shipped out of the country, or how the rustlers always seemed to know which herds were being guarded and which ones weren't.

Finally unable to contain himself, he spoke up. 'Sounds to me like y'all need yourselves a reg'lar range detective.'

All eyes turned to him expectantly. He said nothing. It was, predictably, Oscar Olson who first responded. 'What do you know of this? Who asked for your interference? What do you mean, range detective?'

Robert thought he saw interest quicken in several of the assembled group as a direct result of Oscar's obvious resentment. 'Do you know of such a person?' one of the ranchers asked.

'There's an agency called Pinkerton,' Robert drawled, 'that hires out to solve things like this. They got some fellers workin' for them who are kinda like Texas Rangers, but they work fer Pinkerton, an' they work all over. Not just in Texas. They usually gets deputized wherever they're sent, I guess, and they do a real job.'

'I never heard of such a thing,' Buchanan said.

'I heard tell of it once,' said another rancher, whose name Robert couldn't remember.

'Do you know something about this?' Henry asked.

Robert shrugged. 'Heard tell of it quite a few places. We was up in Wyoming year afore last. They was tellin' up there about a bunch of killin's up around Ten Sleep one time. They sent one of Pinkerton's detectives up there and he solved it, all right. Turned out to be some woman, doin' the killin'.'

'I heard something of that,' another rancher injected. 'Some guy name of Hill. Come to think of it, Walt Hebert was the one tellin' me about it, wasn't you, Walt?'

'Yeah, I was,' a rancher in his late forties responded. He hooked his thumb behind his belt buckle, lifting his paunch a little to allow it. 'Hell on wheels, from what I hear. Levi Hill, his name was.'

'What's it cost to get someone like that sent in?' somebody asked from the yard.

Robert shook his head. 'I ain't got no idee. I reckon it wouldn't cost as much as losin' cattle all the time, though.'

Talk began to erupt in excited buzzes from several places at once. Finally Henry raised his voice above the others, commanding silence. 'Does anyone know how we'd get ahold of these Pinkerton people?'

'They got an office in Cheyenne. Send 'em a wire.'

'Ask the sheriff.'

'Aw he wouldn't know.'

'Well, he might.'

'I think the whole idea is preposterous!' the voice of Oscar Olson rose again. 'The last thing in the world we need is some out-of-state gunman coming in here and accusing everybody in the country. I say we can solve our own problems.'

'Well we haven't got very far yet,' Walt Hebert disagreed. 'And I can't imagine a stranger making more wild accusations than you've been throwing around. I say we should check it out.'

'Oscar, you oughta shut up and get that man of yours home. He took an awful beatin' from that kid.'

'I am not leaving until this meeting is over!' he retorted. 'I'll not stand by and let you men turn this country into a battleground by importing gunmen.'

'A range detective ain't a gunman, Oscar; he's a lawman.'

'If we need a lawman, why ain't the sheriff doin' something?'

'What's he going to do? He's got the whole county to cover. He can't be spending all his time on one thing.'

The conversation broke down again into a ten-way collection of arguments. Robert shook his head and walked back to the tank. He soaked his hands in the cold well water again until he could no longer keep his eyes open. The argument was still raging when he again climbed the ladder to his bed.

5

'So they decided to do it?'

They were in the Hawkinson dining-room. It was the morning after Robert's fight with Hans Lubson and the meeting of the Pine Ridge Cattlemen's Association.

'Yup,' Henry affirmed. 'Only one that was dead set against it was Olson. He's dead set against anything, if he ain't the one that thought of it.'

'Who they goin' to get?' Ralph asked.

'They thought you was recommendin' that Hill, wasn't you, Robert?' the rancher asked.

Robert didn't answer. He was watching Mattie eat. He seemed mesmerized by her movements. The rancher cleared his throat. 'Robert, didn't you say that feller Hill was a good man to get?'

'What?' Robert started out of his

reverie. 'What? Oh, yeah. Well, no, I don't guess I recommended him. He's just one I'd heard of up in Wyoming.'

'Mmm,' the rancher mused. 'Well, they decided to send a wire to Pinkerton's office in Cheyenne and ask for Hill. Time will tell whether they send him or somebody else.'

They finished breakfast and wandered out to the yard. Robert's hands were badly swollen, but he was satisfied nothing was broken, so he largely ignored the pain. He did find several excuses during the day to go to the house and it was always Mattie who came to the door each time he knocked.

I'm afraid that little brother of mine is plumb smitten, Ralph told himself.

They rode out of Hawkinson's place two days later. They had traded away five horses, including the team of percherons. Hawkinson had bought them himself, after trying them out, without quibbling about the price.

They had acquired one new horse, a raw bronc that had belonged to Jack Bertram. 'Had to give ten dollars for 'im,' Robert lamented, 'but he oughta bring twenty or twenty-five easy when we get 'im broke.'

A few miles north they found the edge of timber. The flat land of the high prairie gave way abruptly to a land of buttes, canyons and ridges. It was heavily forested with pine and a few wayward cedar. The canyon bottoms were brushy with chokecherry, wild plum, wild roses and several other kinds of brush. Huge cottonwoods spread their massive branches wherever their roots could reach constant supplies of water. The dusty-looking undersides of their leaves made ripples of changing colour with every shift of breeze.

The effect was breathtaking as they sat their horses along the ridge. It looked like a paradise stretched out before them. Ridge after ridge lay in rows, extending into the hazy distance to the north.

'Now that there's a sudden change o' country,' Robert breathed.

'You reckon them's what they call the Black Hills?' his brother asked.

'Naw, too fur south. Ain't farm country no more, though. That there's cow country, big brother.'

'Forest-fire country if they don't get rain,' Ralph corrected.

They sat their horses there a long time. Robert swallowed, as if to drink the beauty of the land. His eyes reached out to it and let that beauty seep through the dusty layers of his trail-weariness. It felt suddenly to him like a home he had never known, but had been homesick for until just this minute. It was like something he had spent his life searching for, but never even knew he was seeking it.

'A man could sit down in country like that an' never want to leave again,' Robert breathed. Ralph looked at his brother with surprise. 'What d'ya mean?'

'I mean I could stand to stay in a

country like this,' Robert enthused. 'No more wanderin' all over the country. No more horse tradin'. Just sit down and build a ranch and get married and raise a passel o' kids and look out across them hills the rest of my life.'

'Boy, you got it bad, don't ya? I ain't never heard you talk like that afore. You done went an' fell fer that little gal back there, didn't you?'

'What? Oh, well, she's nice right enough. But just look at that country, big brother. Just look at it!'

'Yeah, well, I kinda like Texas myself. Ain't so many trees in the road all the time. C'mon. We gotta get these horses movin'.'

Reluctantly, Robert agreed. He looked out across the country one more time, as if to take in enough of its beauty to sustain him for a long dry spell. With a great sigh he lifted his reins, and they moved the horses along the road, down into the timber.

The next day they corralled their horses in one of a large group of corrals along the railroad track in Chadron, fifteen miles north. They rented a room at the brand-new Blaine Hotel, got their hair cut at a real barber shop and ate two meals at a Chinaman's café on Main Street. They were standing in front of that café just after supper, sucking on toothpicks, feeling prosperous beyond their years or their means. A tall man in a cavalry officer's uniform approached them. 'Are you two the fellows with the horses to trade?'

They came to attention at once. 'Sure thing,' Robert drawled. 'What can we do fer ya?'

'I'm Captain Rogers,' the soldier said. 'From Fort Robinson. Do you know where that is?'

The two brothers looked at each other. 'No, sir, I don't guess we've heard of it,' Ralph responded.

'It's a cavalry base, located some thirty miles west of here,' he announced. 'If you are interested in a lot deal for your horses, I would suggest you take them there. I've stopped by the corral and looked them over. They are all excellent animals. You may tell the quartermaster, a Major Anderson, that I sent you.'

'You mean sell'em all at one time?' Robert asked, the edge of awe evident in his voice.

'Exactly,' the soldier returned. 'The fort has a great need for good mounts.'

'Waal, I don't reckon we ever give no thought to sellin' 'em that way,' Ralph drawled slowly.

'Well, it's up to you. They're your horses. It might be something to consider. The army pays top dollar, in cash,' the officer said. 'Good day, gentlemen.'

He walked away briskly, his back ramrod straight.

'You reckon he knows what he's talkin' about?' Ralph asked.

Robert shrugged his big shoulders. 'Hard to say. Seemed to.'

'That there'd be a purty piece of change, little brother,' Ralph enthused.

'We could head back to Texas right off.'

'Might be a good deal all right,' Robert agreed. ' 'Specially if it don't start rainin' pretty quick.'

The rains did come, though. Ralph and Robert agreed to drive the horses to the fort and try to sell them all. By the time they arrived, they had ridden through rain, snow, mud and biting cold. At last they drove the herd into a corral at the fort and headed for the quartermaster's office. He went at once to look at their horses. Two hours later they were back in his office. He looked through their bills-of-sale carefully, matching them to notes he had made while looking at the horses.

'Well, everything seems to be in excellent order,' he complimented them. 'You do a good job of keeping your papers, having accurate descriptions of your animals, their brands and their previous owners' names. Not all horse traders do this well.'

'We sorta have a thing about not

wantin' to get hung fer horse-thieves,' Robert said.

'That's wise. Well, I'll tell you what the army can do. We can offer you eighteen-fifty each for the twenty-four horses and twenty-one dollars each for the mules. That's if we buy them all, of course.'

Ralph and Robert looked at each other. It was Ralph who spoke. 'You mean you want to pay the same for that roan stallion as you pay for the little pinto?'

The major grinned. 'That's the way the army does things, I'm afraid. The roan is certainly worth more, but the sorrel and white pinto isn't worth nearly that, so it balances out. That's why it hinges on our buying all of them.'

'That'd come to pert near five hundred dollars!' Ralph realized aloud.

'I believe the exact amount would be four hundred eighty-six dollars,' the major corrected.

'We'll take it,' Robert said. Ralph looked at him, then back at the major, then nodded his agreement as well.

The major said, 'I'll need for both of you to sign each of these bills-of-sale, then. How will you want the money drawn?'

'Gold,' both of them responded as one.

The major nodded and walked to the door while they were signing papers. He gave a paper to the sergeant, who disappeared at once. By the time they had finished laboriously signing their names to all the bills-of-sale, the sergeant had returned with a locked metal box. From the box the major counted out their money.

'I would caution you to be quite careful as you leave,' he said. 'It is certainly well known around the fort that you brought horses to sell, so you will be presumed to be carrying quite a lot of money.'

They nodded and returned to the barracks. Dividing the money, they put some in their saddle-bags and some in their pockets.

'Now what do we do, big brother?' Robert said.

'Head for Texas at first light!' Ralph affirmed vehemently.

'I don't know,' Robert hedged. 'I kinda like this country. We could probably hire on with one of them ranchers. Hawkinson mentioned he always has a couple or three hands.'

'Not me!' Ralph asserted. 'I been away from Texas longer'n I ever want to be away from Texas again. At least there I know I ain't gonna get fried one day an' freeze to death in a blizzard the next!'

They argued gently for most of the evening. At first light they were saddled and packed. They stood in the road, looking silently at each other. They had not been apart in all of Robert's seventeen years.

'I sure wish you'd stay,' he told Ralph.

'Yeah, well, I reckon a man's gotta go 'is own way sometime.'

'I got an awful bad feelin' 'bout this,'

Robert confided.

'Yeah, me too,' Ralph agreed. 'Cain't help it though. I'm fer Texas.'

'I know. I just got this awful feelin' I ain't never gonna see you agin.'

They looked at each other in silence for a long moment. Finally Ralph held out a hand. 'Goodbye, little brother.'

Robert grasped the hand tightly, then released it quickly. 'So long, big brother.'

In a moment it was done. The bond that had secured them insolubly to one another over countless miles, through mountains, across rivers, in and out of trouble, was snapped like a thread.

They mounted quickly, both afraid of their own emotions if they tarried. Ralph started south. Robert rode east.

A suffocating weight seemed to settle on to Robert as the distance widened between them, but he refused to allow himself to look back. If he had, he would have seen Ralph sitting his horse in the middle of the road, watching him ride out of sight.

6

It was nearly a month from the time he and Ralph had ridden out of the Hawkinsons' yard until he returned alone. The country was transformed completely. The rains had come. Verdant green had spilled across the country colouring everything in vibrant shades of life. The change almost lifted the lonely cloud of doom that rode with Robert since he and his brother had parted company.

As he rode into the yard he spotted Mattie, and that cloud was suddenly gone. Her smile radiated recognition and joy as he dismounted.

'Why, Robert! I'm so glad you're back. Where's Ralph?'

'Aw, he went back to Texas,' Robert drawled.

'Where are your horses?'

'We done sold 'em all up at Fort Robinson.'

'You didn't go back to Texas with Ralph.' It was a statement, not a question.

'Naw. I sorta like this here country. Thought I might just see if'n your dad needed a hand.'

He was gratified by the sudden rush of pink that tinged her cheeks. He added, 'If'n you don't mind, that is.'

'Well, hello, Robert,' a voice behind him said warmly. It continued as he turned. 'I see you kept the best horse of the string. You sold all the others?'

'Howdy, Mr Hawkinson,' he said, turning and holding out his hand. 'Yessir, we did. Sold 'em all.'

The rancher shook his extended hand warmly. 'Henry,' he corrected. 'You got them all sold in pretty good time.'

'Aw, we just sold 'em all to the army, up at Fort Robinson. Ralph, he done went back to Texas. I was wonderin' whether maybe you was a-needin' a hand?'

'Going to stay around the country, are you? Well, yes, I usually hire on an extra hand about this time. We'll be joining in with the spring round-up, starting the first of the week, then we'll be ploughing some ground I farm, and fencing some more that I want to farm. Then there'll be haying.'

'I, uh, guess I ain't never been around no farmin'.' Robert hesitated. 'I'm a right good hand with cows 'n horses. I could learn, though, I reckon.'

'Fair enough,' Henry said. 'I pay thirty-five a month and your keep the first year. Forty a month after that. There's a third bunk in the bunkhouse. You'll eat with the family.'

Robert marvelled at himself as he moved his things into the bunkhouse. It was the first time since he was a small child he could remember being some place he could call 'home'.

'Yes sir, I just believe I'll be here a while!' he told himself softly. True to his word, Henry had ordered all three hands to join the area's spring round-up. In spite of the biting cold of the early morning, Robert was excited. It was not his first round-up, but it was always a high point of the year in cow country. They rode most of the day to get to Chet Buchanan's place, where it assembled. Jack Bertram's foreman was in charge and gave the orders.

'This is probably about the last year we'll be havin' a round-up all together this way,' he said in answer to Robert's question. 'Country's gettin' too settled. Already too many fences up on the flat. In the canyons and timber there ain't none yet, but they're comin'.'

'Sure lots o' homesteads an' farms an' ranches an' such,' Robert observed.

They were seated in groups near the cook's fire. It was the third day out. They had assembled for a noon meal, which was new to Robert on round-up. He was used to a big meal at breakfast and at supper, but work had always gone on uninterrupted through the noon hour. Here they left a skeleton crew in charge of the assembled cattle and rode to a predetermined site to eat a midday meal together.

'Vel by golly, der vetter ist goot, dis year, anyvay,' Hans DeVeer said.

Hawkinson's other hand sat near him. He was as striking a contrast from the huge Dutchman as could be imagined. Homer Overocker was small, slender and as precise in speech and dress as Hans was awkward. He always wore a round, narrow brimmed bowler hat that stood out like a sore thumb in cow country and either a vest or jacket at all times. Even the dust seemed to avoid him as it settled on everybody else. It was the hat that caused him most of his trouble, though. Such was the case even now.

'You know, I always like to do a little target practice after dinner,' Luke Walker, round-up rep for Walter Hebert's place, said. 'There just ain't nothin' to shoot at.'

Interest picked up as everyone realized something was in the works, but nobody knew what, yet. 'Now take that hat of Homer's,' he continued. Several of the hands began to grin. 'Now that there'd make just a dandy target, if it wasn't sittin' on Homer's head.'

'Well, I dare say,' Homer replied, rising to the bait, 'that it would take a fine shot to hit the bloody thing anyway. I really doubt you're that fine a shot.'

'Aw, I think I could probably hit it at fifty feet or so,' Luke argued.

'Oh I doubt that. I doubt that,' Homer clipped. 'Oh, perhaps if it were sitting immobile, you could, given an adequate amount of time.'

'Hey, I'll tell you what, Homer!' Luke laid out his best trap. 'I just bet I could hit that there hat of yours in mid-air. Matter of fact, I'd just bet a dollar I could.'

'You mean to say that you would be willing to wager a whole dollar that if I throw my hat into the air, you can shoot it before it strikes the ground?'

'Uh huh.'

'Well now, that is interesting. It does seem rather one-sided though, doesn't it? I'll tell you what I will do, Mr Walker; I will accept that challenge and that wager, on the condition that we then reverse the situation.'

'What do you mean,' Luke frowned.

'I mean, that after you have had that opportunity, I will, in turn, have the same opportunity with your hat, for the same wager.'

'You mean you want to shoot at my hat, too?'

'Precisely. If you hit my hat, I will owe you a dollar. If you miss, you will owe me a dollar. Then the same will hold true as I attempt to hit your hat.'

'You're on!' the cowboy chortled. 'Let's just step right over there, and you throw your hat first. I been wantin' a shot at that funny-lookin' thing since you hit the country!'

They stepped to the edge of the area where the hands had assembled. They all came to their feet, and spread out where they could watch. Luke drew his pistol and checked its load. He cocked the hammer. 'OK, Englishman, let 'er fly.'

Homer swept off the hat and soared it, spinning, on a straight line away and to the left. Luke fired frantically, his fourth shot clearly going over the top after the hat had already settled to the ground. Homer calmly walked to where it had landed and retrieved it.

He walked back to the assembled group, dusting it carefully. 'It seems to have escaped your marksmanship unscathed,' he announced.

Luke was livid. 'You didn't throw it right!' he said. 'You was supposed to throw it up, not sail it that way.'

'The agreement merely said I was required to throw it,' Homer corrected. 'I certainly threw it far enough. You fired, I believe, four times. Now, I believe it is my turn.'

'You wanta borrow my gun?' someone called.

'I have my own,' Homer announced. 'I see no reason to carry it obtrusively, but I am armed. Would you care to throw your hat, Mr Walker?'

Luke looked confused for a moment, then shrugged. 'I'll even throw mine the right way,' he said sourly.

He took off his hat and threw it as high as he could throw. Homer's hand came out from under his vest gripping a small .41 calibre Colt. He swung around sideways to the soaring hat, extending his arm straight out, enabling him to sight along the top of the gun barrel. It jumped in his hand six times rapidly. Each time it jumped, the trajectory of the hat shifted. By the time the hat rested on the ground, Homer's hand was back at his side, holding his empty gun.

With a growl, Luke half ran to his fallen hat. Picking it up he turned it over and over, sticking his fingers through the holes in its brim and crown. Stamping his way back to the grinning group of cowboys, he threw it on the ground.

'You set me up!' he yelled. 'You did that on purpose!'

'It seems to me the whole thing was your idea. I believe you owe me two dollars,' the Englishman said, with a perfectly straight face. 'One dollar because you missed my hat and the other because I did not miss yours.'

Luke's face was nearly purple. 'Two dollars! You shot my perfectly good hat plumb full of holes and you think I'm going to give you two dollars to do it? Why you fancy-talkin' little weasel, I'll take you apart!'

His lunge toward the Englishman was brought up short. 'I reckon not,' Robert drawled, as he stepped between them.

Luke brought himself up short, glaring at the intruder.

'This ain't no fight of yours, Texan!'

'Why, it ain't no fight at all,' Robert drawled in response. 'You made a deal, and he stuck by the deal. You got skinnied, all right, but you got took honest. I reckon you oughta just pay up and not be lookin' for a chance to shoot somebody's hat full o' holes next time.'

Luke glared around the assembled group for support, but saw only unanimous grins at his expense. His glare returned to Homer, then to Robert. He dug into his pants and pulled out two silver dollars. He threw them in the dirt. 'You ain't heard the last o' this deal,' he threatened as he stamped off.

'Forty-one Colt,' Robert mused aloud to Homer, as the rest turned to prepare to go back to their work. 'My Uncle Elmer always packed one of them. I always liked a forty-five better.'

'The forty-one is quite accurate, though,' Homer said, 'besides being much lighter to carry. I say it also fits my hand better, which is not nearly so large as yours.'

Robert was not the only one chuckling as they resumed the day's work.

Round-up took just over three weeks. They swept westward from the area past Big Bordeaux Creek. They worked the cattle northward, down out of the canyons and ridges, grouped them, then kept moving westward. When they reached Deadhorse Creek they swung back to the south, ending up with the cattle assembled in one bunch on the prairie, south of the beginning of the timber.

Robert spent all the time he could manage along the rim where the timber began. From here it bore the same exquisite view of ridge after ridge reaching away to the lower elevations to the north. He could just never get enough of the sight.

The reps from the ranches to the south cut out the few of their outfits' cattle that had wandered this far north and headed south with them. Two ranchers from further west did the same. The rest drove the assembled herd eastward, cutting out each outfit's cattle as they passed that ranch. It took another week.

Robert sat on a small rise looking

over the massed cattle. A tight knot in his stomach offered some strange foreboding. It told him more things were about to change than the end of round-up.

7

A new week began with most of the area cattle rounded-up. The assembled herd was being held just above Deadhorse Creek. The tired crew had just finished their evening meal when a lone rider approached the camp.

'Hello the camp,' he called, from outside the light thrown by the cook's fire.

'Hello yourself,' the foreman called back. 'Get down and come in. Supper's over, but I bet the cook can round you up a bite if you're hungry.'

The stranger led his horse into the campfire's glow. 'I'd be obliged,' he said. 'My own cookin' never did keep a lot of meat on me.'

He was of average height, but his legs were much too short for his height. His long body spread out from narrow hips to shoulders that were nearly an axe handle across. He wore the chaps, neckerchief and broad-brimmed, high-crowned hat that marked a Wyoming cowboy. A leather vest hung open, looking much too short for his too-long, powerful torso.

A Winchester .44 lever-action rifle rested in the saddle scabbard. He wore a Colt .45 tied down on his right hip. Extra gear was rolled with his bedroll behind the saddle. A large satchel was tied just behind it. His eyes took in the assembled crew.

'Right good bunch of cattle out there,' he observed.

'Just finishing the area round-up,' the foreman responded. 'Moving 'em back east now, so we can drop off each outfit's cows as we get close. Here's a cup. Coffee's on the fire.'

'Much obliged,' the stranger responded, taking the cup and filling it from the pot on the edge of the coals. 'One of you fellows wouldn't be Jack Bertram or Walter Hebert, by chance?'

Interest quickened around the fire.

'I'm Jack's foreman,' the round-up boss replied. 'Jack ain't ridin' with the crew. Walt Hebert's about due to ride in tonight or tomorrow. His place is down on Deadhorse and his men'll be takin' their cattle that way tomorrow.'

'How's the tally runnin'?' the stranger asked suddenly.

The atmosphere around the fire tensed immediately. There was a painfully long silence before the foreman responded. 'What do you mean?'

'Find as many cows as you should've?' the stranger pursued. 'I understand there's a problem with rustlers in the area. I just wondered if the tally supported that.'

Robert had moved back from the edge of the fire at the first question about the cattle. He had purposely looked off into the night, letting his eyes adjust away from the fire. He moved now where the foreman could see him and know he was ready to back his play if need be.

'I guess I'd like to know who's asking about that,' the foreman said softly.

The stranger glanced around again then back at the foreman. 'I'd be obliged if you'd have your Texan move back over by the fire,' he said just as softly. 'I get kinda nervous when fellas start workin' around behind me.'

The foreman's eyes flicked up to where Robert was standing, then back at the man. 'Who are you?' he asked again.

The stranger said, 'Pinkerton sent me down this way. They said the Cattlemen's Association wanted a range detective to stop the rustlin'. My name's Levi Hill.'

Robert had worked around almost behind the stranger before he heard the name. Levi hadn't quite finished speaking when he stopped. At the mention of his name, there was an audible grunt from one of the crew. Eyes momentarily glanced that way. Robert's eyes did too. Perhaps that's why he never even saw him move.

Suddenly Levi wasn't squatting where he had been. His cup of coffee sat there on the ground. In an instant's panic Robert saw the empty space with the coffee cup, then his feet flew out from under him. He landed with a crash and clawed for his gun, but the holster was empty. He rolled to his feet and sprang to a crouch. Levi was standing behind where he had just been, holding Robert's gun loosely in his right hand.

'Like I said,' Levi said in a calm voice, 'I get kinda nervous when fellas start workin' to get around behind me.'

A ripple of whispered awe swept across the crew. It sounded almost like a wayward breeze that passes across the tops of ripe wheat, then is gone. Every cowboy's hand made a self-conscious move away from its owner's gun.

'How'd you do that?' Robert drawled, awe tingeing his voice.

Levi did not answer. He spun Robert's gun in his hand, twisting it over and handing it butt first back to Robert. Robert swallowed hard but said nothing as he dropped it back into his holster.

'I was askin' about the tally,' he reminded the foreman as he squatted back before his coffee cup. He picked it up, sipping its contents as he eyed the foreman over its rim.

There was another awkward moment, then the foreman said, 'Well, it's kinda hard to say, right off, for sure. But we're short. Aw, we're danged short! I'd make a guess, off the top of my head, that we're probably three hundred head short of what we oughta have right now.'

Levi's eyebrows raised. 'That's a lot of stock to move out of the country without anybody seeing them.'

'That's what's got everybody stumped,' the foreman agreed.

Conversation suddenly erupted from all sides of the fire as the assembled hands began to discuss the favourite topic in the country. Everybody had a theory, but it was quickly apparent nobody really knew anything.

'You mind if I sorta ride along with your outfit?' Levi asked finally.

'Naw, I don't mind,' the foreman said. 'You're welcome. We'd take it kindly if you was to help out a little, as long as you're ridin' along anyway.'

After the rocky start of that first night, he and Robert developed a quick liking for each other. They seemed to think alike, act much alike, and enjoy each other's company.

When the last of the cattle were parcelled out, Levi rode with Robert, Hans and Homer to take the Hawkinson herd home. It was not a large herd. It numbered only a little more than sixty head.

'How come your boss sends all three of you to help on round-up when he ain't got any more cows than that?' Levi asked.

It was Hans who answered. 'Vell, by golly, he tinks dat is der neighbourly ting to do. He has got much more cows den dis, but most of his is sooth of der place und don't get much into der timbers.'

Homer added to the explanation. 'He normally does not send all three of his hands, however. He usually sends Hans or I, but maintains one or two hands at home to help with chores and things. I believe it is because of the feeling of impending trouble he chose to do so this year.'

Levi spent several days helping the Hawkinson hands round-up the rest of their own cattle from the flats. Then they spent one whole day branding. It was hard, demanding work, but always a highlight of every year.

They held the entire herd to one side. The men on horseback would rope the calves as they were ready for them, and drag them to the branding fire. The ones working there would hold the calf down while he was branded, dehorned and, in the case of most of the bull calves, castrated. When they were released, they were allowed to run toward another bunch of cows, held off in the other direction. As each calf went running off, bawling in pain and fear, the mother would break from the holding herd and cross to be with her calf.

'Always amazes me how every cow knows her own calf's beller,' Robert said.

'Any momma knows her own baby's voice,' Henry said. 'I always like watchin' 'em mother up when we're done workin' on 'em. Don't matter what we do to 'em, as soon as they get back with their momma, they're fine.'

Both Mattie and her mother spent the day in the saddle, holding the two groups of cattle. Levi and Robert did the roping. Hans, Homer and Henry worked the calves and the branding fire.

Dining that night on 'mountain oysters', they feasted on the calves' severed pride until they nearly burst.

The next day, armed with descriptions of the places from which cattle were known to have been stolen, Levi rode out for the ridges and canyons of the timber country.

8

'Seems sorta strange to see a Texas cowboy buildin' fence,' Levi said to Robert.

Robert's face reddened, but he said nothing. It was Homer who answered.

'I'm afraid the barbed wires are the thing of the future, Mr Hill. This is a pasture Mr Hawkinson has used previously for his young heifers who are about to calve. Now he wishes it upgraded to hold sheep.'

It had been a week since Levi had ridden out of Antelope Valley. As he returned, he had encountered Hawkinson's three hands working on a long stretch of barbed-wire fence.

'Sheep?' Levi wondered aloud.

'By golly, he does not vish to make the problem vith der neighbours, so he vill fence dem in,' Hans explained.

'Can you make a fence sheep-tight?' Levi asked.

'Oh, yes, by golly, dat is no problem,' the big Dutchman offered. 'Ve is putting two more vires in der fence. Den ve is putting a post between der otter, und a stay betwixt der notter, und it vill hold der sheep mit no problem.'

The explanation made no sense at all to Levi and he started to ask further. Thinking better of it, he contented himself to look at the section of fence already completed, and figure out from that what Hans had said.

He let his horse graze with dragging reins, and talked with the three as they worked. As they went along the fence line, a pair of cottontail rabbits suddenly sprang out of a clump of soapweeds, running and dodging in a broken line. Robert's gun sprang into his hand and jumped twice. Both rabbits fell, twitching. 'Rabbit for supper, boys!' Robert said gleefully.

As he picked up the rabbits and

began cleaning them, Levi joined him. 'Pretty handy with that gun,' he commented, taking one of the rabbits to clean.

'Yeah, thanks,' Robert said. 'My uncle taught me.'

'Who's your uncle?'

'Elmer Blundell.'

'The US Marshal?'

Robert was delighted. 'You know him?'

Levi nodded. 'Met 'im. Small man. Wears a forty-one Colt. Born on a river boat, on the Mississippi, he told me.'

Robert nodded, grinning. 'Grandpa was captain of the *Mississippi Queen*. Uncle Elmer was born on the boat one night, headin' down to New Orleans.'

'Hell on wheels in a fight,' Levi commented.

Robert's grin widened. 'Runs in the family.'

'I might show you something that'd help your draw a little,' Levi said, as they cleaned their hands.

'You mean make me faster?'

'Might. At least, it'll make you a little more sure. I noticed you hold your thumb straight on the hammer when you draw. Sometimes that'll slip off when you go to shoot. That'll make you try twice for your first shot. That could be fatal. Instead, grab your gun so your thumb's crossways on the hammer, like this.'

He took hold of his gun, showing Robert how to grip it. 'Don't that make you slower?' Robert wondered.

'Not after you get used to doin' it,' was the answer.

'Aw, I don't know,' Robert wondered. 'I reckon I'm 'bout as fast as there is already.'

'Actually, you're kinda slow,' Levi disagreed.

Robert's jaw dropped. 'Slow? Slow? You saw me draw 'n shoot them rabbits!'

'Uh huh. That's why I know how slow you are,' Levi answered, eyes twinkling.

'Why, I reckon I'm just as fast as

you are!' Robert blustered.

'Well, I guess you just got to find out, don't you,' Levi grinned. 'Well, let's see. See that soapweed with last year's seed pods standin' on it? We'll have Homer stand behind us, where we can't see 'im. When he's ready, he'll clap his hands. When you hear 'im clap, draw and shoot that seed pod.'

'You're on, Levi!' Robert exulted. 'You wanta lose a dollar on it, too?'

'Save your money,' Levi replied dryly.

They took their positions and waited. Homer clapped his hands. Robert's hand stabbed for his gun. His fingers just closed around the butt when Levi's gun roared. The seed pod flew into the air and fell to the ground.

Robert stood with his gun half out of his holster, mouth agape. He closed his mouth and swallowed hard twice. 'How'd you do that?' he gasped finally.

'I said you was slow,' Levi grinned. 'Wanta try again?'

He did. He tried several more times.

After the second time, he was never allowed to even get a firm grip on his gun butt before Levi's gun spoke.

'You gotta be about the fastest gun what's ever been,' Robert said finally. Levi shook his head. 'There's always somebody faster,' he said. 'That's why you never, ever try to depend on out-drawing someone. That's the reason I showed you this. I ain't tryin' to brag or to show you up. I just don't want you gettin' killed 'cause you thought you were fast.'

They worked together on the fence, then, for a couple of hours. It was Hans who called it a day. 'Vell by golly, ve had best be getting back und cleaned up, if ve is going to der dance tonight,' he announced.

'Dance?' Levi asked.

'Dance over at the school house tonight,' Robert explained. 'I done asked Mattie to go with me,' he added, obvious pride tingeing his voice.

'She said 'no' o' course,' Levi teased.

'What? No!' Robert faltered with

total seriousness. 'She said 'yes'. Why would she say no?'

Levi only chuckled and winked at the other two, who grinned in response, but said nothing.

They ate an early supper, already scrubbed and wearing their best clothes. Robert and Mattie rode in the second seat of the Hawkinsons' buggy, with her parents in front. The rest rode horseback.

Horses, buggies and wagons were tied to every tree and fence post in sight, when they arrived. The school house had been cleared for the occasion. A band, made up of three fiddles and an accordion, was playing lively numbers. The floor area of the school was crowded with couples, keeping time to the music. Some of them danced rather well, he thought. Even his inexpert eye could see that most did not. It didn't matter. They all seemed equally in a holiday mood.

The usual knots of men stood here and there. Some passed a bottle around.

A few groups of women stood about as well, chattering gaily. Children ran and played and yelled at each other.

The dance went on for quite a while, then took a break. During the break Homer stepped up to the band and talked to them in quiet tones for a few moments. They nodded their heads at something, then talked to each other. As people returned from the break, Homer addressed the crowded school.

'I say, we do have a relative newcomer to the area who has a remarkably good voice for singing. He has sung, for Hans and me on occasion. I would like to suggest that we ask Mr Robert Blundell to step forward and sing for us the 'Ballad Of Pattatonia'.'

The crowd began a smattering of applause that quickly grew to a demanding swell. Looking embarrassed, Robert was pushed and crowded toward the band.

He finally relented and talked to the leader of the band in low tones. One of the fiddlers offered a note and Robert nodded. He began in a clear tenor to sing a ballad of a great horse. Each verse ended with the words, 'They called him Pattatonia, the pride of the plains'.

Its many verses told the whole life of the great horse, and there were surprisingly few dry eyes in the audience as the final verse related the great and heroic horse's death. Enthusiastic applause followed him as Robert escaped from the room.

He was just about ready to go back inside when his attention was captured by a circle of men gathered in obvious anticipation. He saw Levi leaning against a tree a short way off, just watching. He walked quickly in that direction.

He entered the circle of men and saw it was Homer who was, once again, the recipient of the antagonism. His antagonist was Luke Walker, still wearing the hat with its unappreciated ventilation holes. He was obviously drunk enough to cloud his judgement, but probably not enough to impair his fighting ability. He was trying to egg Homer into a fight.

Robert stepped into the circle. 'Luke, I already told you, if you have any beef with Homer you can deal with me. He beat you fair and square.'

It was Homer who objected to his intrusion. 'My good man, I certainly appreciate your concern for my well-being, but I assure you this is not your affair. Now kindly step aside and I will deal with this coarse ruffian.'

Frowning, Robert let himself be eased out of the picture. He sidled over to Levi. As he approached, Levi spoke. 'Don't look so worried, Robert. I'd guess that little Englishman's about to surprise a few folks.'

It was that little Englishman who was speaking. 'Mr Walker, are you familiar with the rules of the Marquess of Queensberry, or is this to be a contest devoid of rules?'

'This ain't gonna be no contest,'

Luke growled. 'This is gonna be a beatin'.'

As he spoke, he moved in and swung a surprisingly quick right hook at the Englishman's head. The head wasn't where it should have been, though, and the fist caught only air. In response, the Englishman planted two quick, hard jabs directly on Luke's nose. Blood flew.

Luke roared in anger and followed with a left, then a straight right, both of which missed. They were answered by two more jabs, then a jarring right to the temple.

Luke's left found the Englishman's chin, but was answered with a sudden flurry of blows that left the bigger man confused. For several minutes they circled each other. Luke occasionally landed a decent blow, but for every one he did, he received nearly half a dozen.

Finally deciding he had the Englishman's pattern of movement figured out, Luke swung hard in the direction he thought Homer would move. Instead of trying to avoid the lunging blow, Homer stepped inside of it, close against the big cowboy. A series of rapid punches exploded into the cowboy's midsection. The first drove the wind from him. The several that followed constricted and cramped his abdominal muscles so severely he doubled over helplessly.

The Englishman placed a hand on the back of the stricken cowboy's head and started to step forward, obviously intending to finish the fight with a knee to his face. He stopped with the knee poised. Instead, he just shoved with the hand already on the cowboy's head. Luke toppled over sideways, and lay in the dirt, trying desperately to force his lungs to accept air.

Homer removed the inevitable round bowler from his head, brushing the dust from it carefully. Then he did the same for the rest of his clothes. He walked out of the circle of men looking for all the world like he had just had a pleasant chat over tea. Stares of obvious surprise and approval followed him out of sight.

'That ain't gonna set too well with Hebert,' somebody remarked, as the group broke up. 'That's twice his foreman's been bested by that little Englishman lately.'

'I never did see how come Walt canned old Will and put Luke on as foreman, anyway,' his companion responded.

The first man agreed. 'In the two years since then, I bet Luke's been involved in a fight with eight or ten guys around. That Englishman's the first one who whipped him, though.'

'I hear he's just as handy with a gun as he is with his fists, too.'

'Kinda odd, ain't it? I mean, here's Hawkinson and I can't see as how he really needs three hands. The Englishman turns out to be a regular gunslinger and fighter. Then he hires on this Texan, that's faster 'n better with a gun than anyone in the country who whipped Olson's foreman. How come Hawkinson's gettin' a crew o' fighters?'

'Hadn't thought o' that. Does seem a bit odd, though, just when all this rustlin' starts . . . '

They moved off out of hearing. Robert went back inside to claim another dance with Mattie. Levi continued to wander around, visiting with the different groups of people standing about, but the overheard conversations continued to replay in his mind.

9

The day dawned cloudy and drizzly, with heavier showers erupting periodically. Halfway through the grey, dismal morning, a rider came into the Hawkinson yard. 'Lookin' for the Pinkerton man,' the cowboy said without ceremony.

'I'm him,' Levi responded, coming from the barn.

'Been another bunch o' cattle stole,' he said. 'Jack Bertram sent me up to fetch you. I can show you where.'

'I'll saddle up,' Levi responded.

They rode out together fifteen minutes later. It was a five-hour ride in the intermittent rain. Levi cursed silently when he saw the area. It was a long valley, protected on all sides by the forested hills. The tall thick grass would show few tracks, if any. There were roads that went by on both sides of the valley, allowing small bunches of cattle to be moved, at night, with little chance of detection. The rain that had followed would have already wiped out any trace of tracks.

'No way in the world to track 'em,' he said aloud.

'Same every time,' the cowboy agreed. 'They hang back and wait for a storm to come. They always hit just ahead o' one, then the rain wipes out their tracks.'

'Well I guess it's time I visited with the rest of the ranchers,' Levi said. 'How long's it take to call a meeting of the Cattlemen's Association?'

'Oh, couple, three days.'

'Where do they usually meet?'

'Oh, any o' the ranches, I guess. Olson's, lot o' the time. He's got lots o' room. Buchanan's is more central, though.'

'OK. Let's have 'em meet at Buchanan's, day after tomorrow evening. I'm going to ride on into Chadron and do some more nosing around.'

★ ★ ★

When he rode into Buchanan's yard, he saw the Cattlemen's Association had turned out in force. 'Looks like quite a gathering,' he muttered to his horse.

He was introduced around. Three faces in the crowd were openly hostile: Oscar Olson and his foreman and Luke Walker. Some were just as openly friendly. The rest were guarded and neutral. He was introduced.

'You'd just as well know, Hill, I think it's nothing but a waste of money having you here,' Oscar Olson asserted, before anything else could be said, or any discussion started.

The belligerence of his effort was not well received. A smattering of low mumblings rippled across the room. 'Aw, let him speak his piece, Oscar,' someone said aloud.

'Well, we don't need him!' Oscar argued. 'We already know some of the ones who have to be involved. I say we can watch them and we can handle this thing by ourselves.'

'You think you know some who are involved?' Levi asked.

Oscar cleared his throat. He looked around at the others, then back to Levi. 'Well, I suppose we can't be certain, but real close to certain. Take that Texas gunman out at Hawkinson's. He's a perfect example.'

Levi's eyebrows shot up. He waited, but Oscar offered nothing further, so he asked, 'What makes you think he's involved?'

'Well, think about it! He comes ridin' through here with a string o' horses he don't want nobody seein' papers on . . . '

'He showed us the bills-o'-sale, Oscar,' someone's voice interrupted, exasperation clearly showing in the tone.

'Yeah, he showed 'em to you, but he didn't show 'em to me. He beat my foreman half to death, and I ain't never known anybody could beat him at all let alone like that. Then he just happens to know where he can sell that many horses all at once. Now that's suspicious.'

'The army's always lookin' for horses, Oscar,' Jack Bertram said. 'They've even been out to my place a time or two, askin' about whether I had any I'd be willin' to sell 'em.'

'How about cows?' Oscar insisted. 'The same thing oughta apply to cows, hadn't it? And if he knows the quartermaster well enough to sell him horses, do you think he can't sell him cows just as easy? It just doesn't make sense that he's in this country for any other reason, I tell you! He's a first-rate gunman! I heard guys say they've seen him draw and shoot a runnin' rabbit in the eye so quick you can't even see him move! I saw him do the same with a prairie chicken myself! Shot him right out of the air! Hit him in the head, he did.'

'The fact that a man's good with a gun doesn't mean he's a thief,' Levi said quietly.

'Maybe not, but it's a good place to start,' Oscar insisted.

'Now, Oscar,' the calm voice of Walt Hebert prevailed. 'I know how upset all this has you. It does all of us. But you can't accuse a man without any evidence. We've hired an investigator. Let's let him do his job.'

'Least you can do is arrest that Texan,' Oscar insisted. 'Lock him up in Chadron till you check him out.'

Several voices objected at once. Olson listened to the gist of the comments long enough to ascertain he had no support whatever among the assembled ranchers. He finally threw up his hands in exasperation.

Levi took advantage of the resulting lull to focus the group's attention in a new direction. 'Which of you had new hands hire on within six months of when the rustling first started?' he asked.

They all looked at each other in evident puzzlement, so he explained. 'It's not likely, in a country this settled, that a bunch of outlaws is hiding out in the hills. It's more likely they're working on different places. That way, they know when there's cattle in a good spot to steal.'

The suggestion created a stir of enquiries and conjecture, but little of substance. In fact, the meeting produced little Levi didn't already know. The rustlers seemed to know what bunches of cattle wouldn't be watched, and always picked off a small bunch, never more than twenty head or so, just before rain or snow obliterated all tracks.

The meeting ended two hours later and those attending began to ride off in groups of two and three. Levi also left. He rode away with the feeling this was going to be more difficult than he had expected.

10

Robert's steps showed even more bounce than usual. He was decked out in his finest clothes, his hair was carefully combed beneath his well-brushed hat and his boots showed obvious hard work with saddle soap.

He showed Mattie to the buggy. 'Boy, it sure is good of your dad to let us take the buggy, all by ourselves,' he exulted.

Mattie smiled self-consciously. 'Especially clear over to Ash Creek,' she agreed. 'I've never been to a dance over there.'

Robert had asked for permission to take Mattie there and for the use of the buggy, with little real hope of getting to do so. When Henry agreed, he was beside himself with glee.

They started the six-hour trip in early afternoon. They stopped at a small spring about halfway to water the horses and spread out a blanket and picnicked while the horses rested, then resumed their trip. Mattie chattered cheerfully all the way. Robert didn't want to ever get there. He knew when the dance started, he would have to share her and it was not a welcome prospect.

They arrived with the first of the celebrants and Mattie found she knew far more people than she anticipated. As Robert had dreaded, there was a constant line of partners waiting for a dance with her. She saved every other dance for Robert, though, and he was walking on air.

Even when a young man walks on air, nature must be accommodated. Finally, while Mattie was dancing with one of the Buchanan boys, he slipped outside to relieve himself in the timber. He wasn't clear back inside when he heard the uneasy silence. As he entered the door, its cause was immediately apparent.

Three drifters had put in an appearance in the area with the coming of spring. They were rough customers and stuck together like glue. One was a huge man.

'Uglier than a mud fence plastered up with toads,' one woman described him.

The other two were smaller, but just as dirty, ugly, and mean. The smallest of the three was addressing Mattie where she was cornered against one wall.

'Now, little lady, we done asked you to dance, so we's goin' to dance with you. Matter o' fact, I 'spect we's just gonna spend the rest o' the dances adancin' with you. Now, unless you want some o' these good folks to get hurt, real bad, you best just come dance.'

By the time he had finished his little speech, Robert was at Mattie's side. He didn't speak. He just sent a crashing right hand full into the man's dirty smile. Blood flew like juice from a squashed tomato. The other two responded immediately. Robert fought like a cornered wildcat, using fists, elbows, knees, feet, and his head. Slowly, however, the three battered him down.

Finally the biggest of the three got behind Robert and wrapped his arms around him. Robert leaned back into him, pounding the back of his head repeatedly into the man's face. In spite of the pounding, the big man held on, and the other two started driving crushing blows into the pinioned cowboy.

Whether the crowd would have come to his aid or let him fight his own fight is impossible to determine. They all knew who he was. They all knew he had the reputation of a fighter and a gunman: they also knew that many entertained suspicions of his association with the rustlers.

Suddenly there was a sodden 'thunk', and the arms holding Robert relaxed. The big man dropped to the ground like a sack of wet noodles and did not move. Suddenly freed, Robert tore into the other two with a fury like nothing Mattie had ever seen. He quickly knocked one man unconscious, then missed with a looping left at the one who had been speaking to Mattie when he had returned. Rather than with-drawing the fist, he let it continue, wrapping it around the man's dirty neck.

With a jerk he pulled the man's head downward, locking him in a vice with his head held against Robert's side. With his free right hand, Robert began to pound the face he held immobile with all the pent-up fury of a caged bull.

His arm was aching when a familiar voice said, 'I reckon that's enough, Robert.'

He looked up into Levi's face. His fist, poised to deliver another blow to the drifter's face, was held in Levi's vice-like grip. Blinking, he looked down. The drifter was completely unconscious, hanging limply, his head still locked in Robert's grip. His face was an unrecognizable mass of raw meat. Robert blinked several times again, slowly becoming aware of his surroundings. The drifter slid from his grasp, landing in a small pool of his own blood and lying still.

Levi spoke to Mattie as he put an arm around Robert's shoulder. 'I'll go get him cleaned up a bit, ma'am. He'll be back in a few minutes.'

To the crowd, still watching silently, he spoke more loudly. 'How about some of you fellows draggin' these three out an' throwin' 'em in the crick for a while. That'll cool 'em off, and maybe wash 'em just a little. Can't see that either one would hurt much. Let's get this dance goin' again.'

There was a ripple of nervous laughter at his comments, and several men stepped forward to clean the carnage from the floor. Two of the women finally rushed to Mattie's side, offering her some belated help and comfort. Levi eased Robert outside and headed him for the creek as well.

'You the one who knocked the guy off my back?' Robert asked, after the cold water had produced a measure of benefit.

'Yeah, I sorta thought it might help the situation. I just wrapped my gun barrel around his head a little. Hope I didn't bend it!'

Robert scrubbed the residue of battle from his hands and face and, as best he could, from his clothes. They were not yet back to the school house when Mattie found them.

'Oh, Robert, are you all right?' She reached for him and his arms went around her, surprised to find her trembling against him.

'Oh, Robert, I was so afraid! They were so big, and so dirty, and nobody was doing anything to help me, or then to help you, and I thought they were going to kill you! Oh, Robert, please take me home.'

As Levi escorted them to their buggy,

he over-heard the usual remarks from gathered knots of people.

'By jing, he didn't go for his gun, even then.'

'Sorta gets wound up when he loses his temper.'

'Didn't hesitate a minute to take on them guys when his girl was in trouble.'

'Shoulda been in there helpin' 'im, that's what we shoulda been.'

Robert helped Mattie to the seat, untied the team, and climbed up beside her. Then a thought suddenly occurred to him. 'What are you doin' here?' he asked.

'Just nosin' around,' Levi grinned. 'You sorry I showed up and spoiled your fun?'

'Much obliged to you for pitchin' in,' Robert drawled, beginning to recapture his ebullient good nature. ' 'Course, I coulda handled it all right, but I might have gotten mad and really hurt them fellas.'

Levi waved a hand and turned away.

'Watch yourself,' he called over his shoulder.

Robert did that, watching and listening much closer to his surroundings than he had on the way over. It was in the small hours of the morning when they pulled into the Hawkinson yard. Mattie had been asleep against his shoulder for the past two hours. For the second time that day he had the feeling he really didn't want the moment to end.

It was late afternoon the next day when Oscar Olson and two other ranchers rode into the Hawkinson yard. They rode directly to the house and dismounted without ceremony. Henry had stepped outside to meet them.

'Well, get down and come in, men,' he said, even though they were already down.

'Henry,' Olson barked, 'that hired gunman o' yours has been at it again. This time it was at the dance over on Ash Creek; he started a fight. Busted up the whole place. It's gettin' so this country can't even have a dance any more without one or another of your hired gunmen making a battleground out of it. We want him out of the country!'

'Well now, that's quite a mouthful,' Henry said, looking from one to the other. 'Not only that, it's quite a different story from what I got from my daughter, as well as a couple other people who were there.'

'Are you denying he was in another fight?' Olson demanded.

'I'm denying he started a fight,' Hawkinson said, refusing to back down an inch. 'He came to my daughter's defence, as any decent man should have done. Which is something I'd like to ask you, Oscar Olson: your foreman was over at Ash Creek, at that dance and he didn't lift a finger to help my daughter. She was cornered by three of the dirtiest drifters to hit this country for several years and your foreman kept out of it. Why, Oscar? Why was your foreman over at Ash Creek? Why isn't he man enough to help a girl in trouble?'

Oscar's face was turning redder by the minute. 'Now you listen to me, Henry, don't you go trying to shift the subject. We're talking about that gunslinging rustler you got working for you, and that's all we're talking about!'

'Who you callin' a rustler?' a voice drawled softly from the corner of the house.

All eyes swivelled to Robert, standing with his left hand against the corner of the house, his right suspended above his gun butt. Nobody moved. Nobody spoke.

'I heard somebody called a rustler. Is there somebody here who wants to tell me to my face he thinks I'm a thief, or that I'm involved with the cattle thieves?'

Nobody moved. Nobody spoke.

That same quiet drawl, pregnant with deadly anger, continued. 'Oscar Olson, I'm calling you a fat-faced, loud-mouthed pig. I'm saying you've got the biggest mouth and the littlest brain in Nebraska. I'm calling you to either back up your words or turn around and run like the yellow-bellied polecat you are.'

Olson's face had gone from its fiery red to pale, to pasty white. He swallowed audibly. He finally found his voice, but it squeaked as he spoke. 'Now look, I ain't accusin' you o' being no rustler.'

'You already did,' Robert insisted in that same quiet drawl. 'Now either back it up or turn tail and run.'

'Now you ain't gonna prod me into drawin' on you,' Oscar said, beginning to recover some of his bluster. 'I'm no gunman. I ain't got no use for gunmen either. This country'd be a whole lot better with the likes of you gone.'

'Get off my place, Oscar,' Henry said. 'You ain't welcome any more. Art, Matt, I ain't heard nothin' out of you. If you agree with Oscar, you ain't welcome either. If you don't, then you are. I'm askin' where you stand.'

'He didn't have any right to say

those things,' Art said. 'All we heard was Oscar's version. That don't sound nothing like what your daughter says. I guess if I got to make a choice, I'll believe Mattie. Fine girl she is.'

'I'll go along with that,' Matt agreed. 'Oscar, why don't you just ride on home alone and think about having that jaw bone of yours wired shut for a while.'

With the immediate threat to his life gone, Oscar's complexion returned to its normal angry red. 'Some fine friends you two turn out to be,' he stormed as he stamped to his horse and mounted. 'It's a sorry day in this country when some two-bit gunman can come in and set friends against friends. It'll be a good day when somebody pats that Texas saddle tramp in the face with a shovel and I don't care who hears me say it.'

He was still muttering to himself as he jammed spurs to his horse's sides and rode stiffly from the yard. Robert turned without a word and went to start the evening chores.

The next evening, Robert and Mattie walked into the house, hand in hand. They had asked permission to walk in the grove behind the house and returned aglow with the flush of young love. Henry's eyebrows raised at their boldness, walking right into the house holding hands. Esther followed them from the kitchen, forehead furrowed, hands buried in her apron. They stopped before Henry.

'Mr Hawkinson,' Robert drawled. 'I'd like to ask your permission, and Mrs Hawkinson's too, I reckon, to court your daughter. I want you to know, my intentions are honourable.'

Henry stood slowly and his wife rushed to his side. They looked from one to the other, then at each other. Finally a slow grin started across Henry's face. 'Well, young man, I guess I ain't nowhere near ready for this! I know, Mattie's a young woman now, but nobody's asked to court her before. I, well, what are your plans?'

'Well, sir, we've been talking quite a lot. It ain't like we're gettin' engaged or nothin'. Not yet. But that there is what we got in mind. I got quite a bit of money laid by from horse tradin' an' all. 'Tain't enough to start up a place yet, but I reckon it ain't goin' to take too long afore we can start thinkin' about our own place.'

Henry and his wife exchanged looks again. The furrows in Esther's forehead were slowly being replaced by crinkles at the corners of her eyes. 'I think it's very nice of you to ask to court Mattie, Robert,' she said. 'You have my permission.'

'Now see that?' Henry asked. 'You take note of that, Robert. Any man that says he makes the decisions in his own house will probably lie about other things too!'

The tension dissolved. The mood immediately changed to one of celebration. Robert's and Mattie's eyes were filled with each other for the whole evening.

11

Robert rolled out of his bunk and dressed quickly, feeling euphoric. Life was good. He could not remember being happier. He had a job. He had a girl. He had a prospect of a whole life suddenly spread before him. He saw within his grasp the fulfilment of every hope and dream he had ever dared to hold.

He went to the house with the other hands for breakfast. Mattie was, as usual, helping her mother feed the crew. Everything she brought to the table, she brought to where Robert was sitting. She brushed against him and laid a hand on his shoulder every time she set something on the table. Every touch sent another electric thrill through Robert's whole being. Not sure why, he struggled to keep those feelings from being obvious to the rest of the crew. He need not have bothered. Everyone in the room was fully aware of those feelings.

After breakfast, Henry called Robert aside. 'Robert, I've got that one bunch of three-year-olds that are pastured out north and east. Hans was out that way yesterday and saw nothing of them. They may have wandered over toward Spring Canyon, or even over toward Bordeaux Creek. I'd like for you to take a couple of days and see if you can spot them. Haze them back on to our own place pretty well, and let them spread out again. If they're closer to the big windmill than they are to other water, they shouldn't wander too far.'

'You think they're there?' Robert responded, trying to decipher the uneasiness in Henry's tone.

'Well, if it wasn't for all the rustlin', I wouldn't think anything of it. They wander quite a ways, sometimes. But under the circumstances, it wouldn't hurt to check. You, uh, watch yourself, you hear?'

That last admonition rang a note of alarm in Robert's head. It sparked a tight feeling in the pit of his stomach he couldn't decipher. It reminded him of what he had felt as he and Ralph rode away from each other. He left an hour later. He rode a series of long zigzags throughout the day but found no trace of the cattle.

He descended into the cool shade of the timber and found a small spring trickling out of the side of a canyon. Tracks of several cattle, only a few days old, brightened his mood. Looks like I came the right way, he told himself.

That nagging premonition of warning, so persistent when he left Hawkinson's, was not so noticeable. Maybe he just wasn't listening to it. He should have been.

The trail of the cattle he was seeking was getting fresh. Flies were just beginning to gather on the droppings. He knew he should start seeing some of them any moment.

A flash of sun on metal caught his

attention at the rim of the canyon he had just entered. He started to stand in his stirrups to try to see it again. As he did, the feeling of imminent danger returned. Alarms sounded in his head. He caught his breath and started to dive from the saddle.

He was too slow. Before he could move, he was knocked from the saddle by a sudden blow to the chest. The ground hit him with stunning force, as the sound of a shot reached his ears.

He tried to get up off the ground, but felt like he was held there by some great weight. He tried to cry out, but something seemed stuck in his throat, so he could not. Then he tried to turn his head to see what had struck him, but his head was too heavy to move.

Some kind of darkness was moving in from the edges of his vision on both sides. It kept coming until only a small circle of light remained right above him. He tried to speak, but nothing came. He tried to feel his body to see what was wrong, or to find some pain to tell him what was happening, but he couldn't move his hands; he couldn't move anything at all. The small circle of light separated into two circles, then they both slowly closed above him and he felt himself drift into a darkness he couldn't even feel.

He didn't even realize his shattered heart, that he had pledged to Mattie, was no longer beating. He and Mattie had spent the recent days dreaming so many dreams together. He didn't even feel them die.

12

'Evening, Miss Hawkinson.'

'Hello, Levi. Levi did you see Robert anywhere?'

'Robert? No ma'am. Was I supposed to see him?'

'No. Well, I was hoping maybe you had. I'm sorry! I'm forgetting my manners. Won't you come on up to the house and stay for supper?'

'I was sorta hopin' to be asked,' Levi grinned.

The rest of the family seemed as preoccupied at supper as Mattie. It was Henry who finally explained. 'You ain't been over north-east, by chance, have you?'

'No. I've been nosin' around over toward Deadhorse Crick. Why?'

'Well we've been getting some worried over Robert. Hans said he didn't see that bunch of three-year-old heifers we

118

had over north-east when he was up that way. I sent Robert to check on 'em, and haze 'em back up toward the big windmill. As long as there's water there, they don't generally wander too far off. Anyway, it's been more'n a week now and he ain't come back.'

Levi looked from face to face, seeing the concern and fear echoed from each. 'I'll ride out that way first thing in the morning,' he said.

The threat of the sun's approach was sufficient to begin driving the dark shadows into hiding as Levi rode out of the yard the next morning. He was well out of sight of the buildings by the time it emerged from behind the horizon.

Robert's tracks were a week old, but Levi's uncanny eye could still pick out tell-tale marks of his passing. He was confused at the first couple of zigzags Robert had made, but quickly figured out what he was doing. That made trailing him quicker. Instead of following his tracks, he kept on in the general direction the younger man was going. He reassured himself each time he crossed the trail that he was still on course. When Robert had picked up the trail of the missing cattle, he had their trail to follow as well.

Levi noted with satisfaction the way Robert had followed the cows' sign and ridden directly the way they were wandering. 'Bet he found 'em all less than a half a day from the time he left here,' he said.

An uneasiness began to grow deep inside him with the thought. 'So where's he been since then?' he muttered.

An hour later he spotted a buzzard as he descended behind a ridge. As he topped out the edge of the next canyon he saw several magpies in the tops of trees near the centre of the canyon bottom. That uneasy feeling clamped his stomach in an iron grip of premonition. Sensing his rider's concern, the horse's ears shot forward. Then he lifted his head and nickered. An answering nicker came from the canyon bottom. A moment later Robert's horse appeared, reins dragging.

Levi held back his horse, forcing him to walk slowly. He studied every detail of trees, ground, rock and skyline as he approached. His mind already knew what lay ahead, but his heart refused to hear the words. At the canyon bottom, the trees and brush fell away, leaving the bottom land deep in rich grass. A flock of magpies and three buzzards were glutting themselves on something hidden by the grass's height.

Still scanning the rims of the canyon, Levi rode close enough to see. A cold fire of anger sparked in the centre of his being. It grew, spreading that icy heat through him as he took in the scene.

Robert's body lay on its back. His eyes and much of his face was gone, eaten away by the birds. The centre of his chest was likewise gone. As Levi watched, a magpie crawled out of the hole and waddled away, too stuffed to fly.

Levi fiercely tore open the rolled bundle behind his saddle. He whipped out a Colt revolving shotgun and stepped down from his horse. Holding the gun at hip level, he approached Robert's body. The shotgun began to fire so rapidly it sounded almost like a continuous roar. Black and white magpies, buzzards and feathers flew in all directions. Some kept going in wild panic, while others only cartwheeled back to earth. They would lie there until they, themselves, began to sate the remorseless appetite of their fellows.

With the shotgun empty, Levi stood beside the body, trembling with anger. He wheeled back and caught up Robert's nervous horse, dragging him by the reins as close to the fetid body as the horse would allow. He took down Robert's bedroll. Removing its ground tarpaulin, he spread it beside the body.

Steeling himself against the rising tide of nausea at the stench of the bloated corpse, he tried to roll it over on to the tarpaulin. The nausea won.

When he had emptied the contents of his stomach and retched until his body finally relaxed, he returned to the grisly task. This time he succeeded in rolling the body onto the tarpaulin. He tucked both ends in securely as he rolled. Then he took Robert's lariat from his saddle and lashed the tarpaulin securely.

'Guess I'd just as well get him loaded while I'm at it,' he muttered. He took a blanket from Robert's bedroll and covered the tarpaulin with it, making one more layer between himself and the fetid corpse. Then he wrapped his arms around it and hoisted it to his shoulder.

The horse shied away, refusing to accept the grisly burden. Swearing, Levi lowered it to the ground again. He caught the horse's reins, leading him to the nearest tree and tied him close, allowing him no room to shy away, then returned and hoisted the body again.

This time the horse had no choice, but his dancing and snorting clearly expressed his disapproval of the gruesome burden. When the body was laid across the saddle, it was too stiff to bend over the saddle. He tied it that way, sticking out each side like a rolled up log. Levi walked away. 'Reckon I'll have to bury these clothes,' he lamented. 'Never going to get the stink out of 'em.'

His own horse confirmed the fear and Levi, uncharacteristically, swore again as he lunged to catch the trailing reins. 'Guess he won't mind waitin'' while I see if I can find where he got shot from,' he told the horse.

He rode directly to the rim of the canyon. He hadn't given it any conscious thought. He just knew from long training and sign he didn't even realize he was reading, the direction from which the shot had come. He was rewarded at once with tracks at the canyon rim.

He dismounted. Everything faded

from his consciousness except what lay in front of him. The anger, the stench, the nausea, the grief, all receded behind a curtain of his mind, leaving him in total concentration.

He saw the tracks where someone had waited. He saw the spent brass of the cartridge. He saw the impression of the man's knee where he knelt to shoot. He saw the man's actions as he watched to be sure he had accomplished his task. He saw the absence of any haste in the way he mounted his horse and rode away.

Levi dismounted and picked up the spent brass. 'Forty-four forty,' he muttered.

Pocketing the brass, he remounted and followed the fleeing trail of the killer. He followed it easily north and east. An hour later, the trail turned on to the road leading south-east. He followed the trial for nearly a quarter mile down the road until it became too badly obliterated by random traffic to pick out.

Without a word he wheeled and returned to the body and the panicked horse who bore it. The horse's hatred of his burden did not lessen as they set out, but he tolerated it. If he'd had a choice, he'd have gone his own way and pretended the body was never there. So would Levi.

13

Both horses' steps lagged. They were both too tired to care what they bore. Levi reeled in the saddle. Topping a low rise, he finally approached Hawkinson's yard. It was past midnight, but a lamp still burned in the window. Dogs began to bark while Levi was barely in sight of its glow. Before he reached the yard the dogs had both fallen silent, whining softly at the sombre message borne on the wind.

Levi heard Henry call over his shoulder from the front door as he approached. By the time he pulled up before the door, all three Hawkinsons were standing, huddled together, fighting against what they already knew.

The bunkhouse door slammed, and Hans and Homer came across the yard.

'It's Robert,' Levi said simply.

'Noo!' An anguished wail broke from Mattie's throat. She started for the horses, but Levi stopped her. 'Ma'am, I don't think you want to go out there. He was . . . he was . . . dead for a couple days before I found him. I reckon the best thing is to not get too close.'

She emitted another wail and turned to her mother. Esther led the sobbing girl back into the house. Henry said nothing. He stared at Levi, waiting. The muscles at the hinge of his jaw bunched rhythmically. His teeth never relaxed their clench.

Levi sighed heavily. 'He got about fourteen miles on east and someone shot him. He never moved after he hit the ground. Shot him in the chest with a forty-four forty, from about a hundred yards.'

'You track him?'

Levi nodded. 'Far as I could. He met up with that road that goes south and east. I lost his trail a ways up the road.'

'Olson.'

'What?'

'Olson,' the rancher breathed again. 'He said we'd be patting him in the face with a shovel.'

'Olson threatened him?'

Henry told him then about the confrontation Robert had with Olson shortly before going in search of the cattle. 'I really didn't think Oscar was that kind of a man,' he lamented. 'Guess I was wrong.'

'Don't be too sure.'

'Why? You know something you ain't sayin'?'

'No, but I don't know that Olson did it, either.'

'How much proof you want? Listen, Levi, that boy was gettin' to be like one of my own. I thought maybe he was going to be that son I never had. Now he's gone, just because he wouldn't stand around and let that pompous jackass accuse him of being a rustler! It's about as cut and dried as it can get.'

'Things ain't always what they seem at first,' Levi insisted. 'I'll talk to Olson, but I ain't convinced he done it.'

Hans and Homer did not speak or interfere as Levi tried to stem the fiercely rising tide of the rancher's quiet but deadly anger. He finally wrung a grudging promise from him not to seek his own vengeance until Levi had had the opportunity to investigate the murder.

Reluctant to allow the merciless sun another day to fester the already ripe corpse, the four men went together to the knoll behind the house. They dug a grave there, beside two others. One bore the marker of a child the Hawkinsons had lost at birth. The other was of a hand killed by lightning several years before.

When it was finished, they brought the body, laying ropes under it to allow it to be lowered. They summoned the women. They lowered the body as gently as possible into the hole, still tightly wrapped in the feeble protection of the ground tarpaulin. Hans offered a simple prayer and the shovels began to work, to the accompaniment of Mattie's violent sobs, until the job was done.

At daylight, Levi was in the saddle again. He camped at a spring that night, then spent the next morning scouring the area around where Robert had also camped. He wanted to know if the killer had stalked him, or if it was only a chance encounter that afforded the opportunity. He found no sign of anyone's presence.

Then he rode to the spot from which Robert had been shot. He backtracked the killer to see where he had come from. Within a couple of miles he found the cattle Robert had been seeking. He also found the killer's sign, on the canyon rim above where they were grazing.

The cattle had found a lush area of deep grass and good water and appeared perfectly content to stay put.

Levi found sign where the killer had returned several times, watching them from the canyon rim, then riding away without disturbing them. He had been back twice since Robert was shot. 'Just bad dumb luck Robert rode into his sights,' he seethed.

Some part of his mind noted a line of clouds in the south-west as he rode down into the canyon. 'Looks like a change in weather,' he noted idly to himself.

He rode back to a small spring and made camp again. He had been asleep for a couple of hours when he came suddenly awake with the clarity of midnight insights. He scurried out of his blankets, rolled his belongings and saddled his horse. He was nearly finished when he heard the unmistakable sounds of cattle moving.

He mounted up silently. Following the sound he moved quietly in that direction. A full moon came up, bathing everything in the soft edges of an eerie white light. He pulled up, listening and trying to remember details of the land the cattle were moving through. He probed his mind for details he should have automatically noted as he had ridden through. Best wait till they get over that next ridge, he told himself. If I follow along, maybe I can find out where they're taking 'em.

He listened into the night until he was satisfied the last of the cattle were well ahead. He nudged his horse, and noted with appreciation that Smoky always seemed to understand when he needed to walk quietly. He topped the ridge and started down into the next canyon when his horse's ears pricked up suddenly. Levi dived from the saddle, even as a gunshot pierced the night.

From the corner of his eye he saw the flash from the hidden gun as he dived. He hit the ground and rolled as a second bullet kicked up dirt beside him. He came to his feet and lunged sideways as a third shot buzzed angrily past his ear. His gun was in his hand and he fired three quick shots, one directly at the flash of the other's gun and one about two feet to either side.

He was rewarded with the unmistakable 'thwack' of a bullet penetrating flesh. He hit the ground again, and rolled behind a bush. He heard several small, strangled sounds from the direction in which he had shot, then nothing. He watched his horse, standing in the moonlight, but he appeared to have lost interest.

He gathered his feet under him and lunged suddenly from his cover. He ran in a broken line to another clump of brush fifty feet to his right. There was no response. He tried the same tactic again, diving for cover behind a fallen tree. Again there was no response.

He circled then, moving quietly, to approach his assailant's position from the other side. He was nearly there when he saw the feet. One had the toes pointing straight up. The other was doubled backward, the foot bent back at about a thirty-degree angle. Seeing no movement for a long while, Levi approached warily. Vacant eyes were busy returning the moon's mindless stare.

Levi stood looking down at him. One of the guys Robert whipped at Ash Crick, he noted silently. He ain't the one that shot 'im, though. Wrong tracks. Wrong gun. Well, that gives us another couple of people to talk to about it, anyway.

He took the man's weapons and returned to his horse. He sought out the other man's horse, and removed the bridle. Looping the reins so they wouldn't drag, he fastened the bridle to the saddle horn. 'I'd like to follow you to see where you go home to,' he told the horse, 'but that might take several days.'

Mounting again, he set out cautiously on the trail of the stolen cattle. He followed them most of the night. They continued almost due west, swinging wide around Chet Buchanan's place.

Know the country all right, Levi admired.

The line of approaching clouds overtook the moon's path, and the night grew dark. It became increasingly difficult and dangerous for Levi to track the fleeing rustlers, but he clung tenaciously to the task. It was past two in the morning when their tracks merged into the road that headed north toward King Canyon and the lower country beyond. The wind was beginning to pick up. The promise of rain was in the air. Never going to catch up with them now, before the rain wipes out their tracks again, he lamented.

He followed the road anyway. 'Guess I'd best ride on into town and tell the sheriff what's happened,' he told his horse.

The rain began with daylight. He unrolled his slicker and donned it, riding in the rain all the way to Chadron.

14

Daylight found Levi in the saddle again, visiting ranches in a wide circle. Every rancher he talked with had lost cattle. Some had lost only a few; some had lost nearly half their herd. Every bunch had been driven off just ahead of rain or snow. By the time they were missed, the trail was always obliterated. The only exceptions were those living close enough to a major road. The cattle had simply been moved along the road where their tracks were obliterated by normal traffic.

As he worked his way over into the Deadhorse area, he stayed over at Walt Hebert's. He was impressed with the careful maintenance of the house, the yard, and the buildings. 'Fine spread you've got, Walt,' he admired.

'Been real lucky,' Walt disclaimed. 'Things have gone good for us here.'

'Lived in the country long?'

'Pert near twenty-five years,' was the answer. 'Came up from Missouri just after we was married.'

They were interrupted by a very pretty young lady who stepped out of the house. 'Supper time, Papa,' she called.

Walt waved her over to them. 'Levi, this is my oldest daughter, Naomi. Naomi this is Levi Hill, the range detective I've been talking about.'

Levi looked into the dancing blue of the biggest eyes he had seen in a long time. They looked like a deep sea filled with the currents of countless hidden promises. He thought a man could swim there for a lifetime. He held out his hand. 'Miss Hebert, happy to meet you.'

'Please call me Naomi,' she smiled, taking his hand in a surprisingly strong grip. 'Will you come and eat with us?'

'I'd be obliged,' he responded at once.

'You'd just as well put your horse

up and stay the night,' Walt invited.

He didn't need to ask twice. Levi enjoyed that supper more than he had any meal he'd eaten in Nebraska. Walt and Molly Hebert had two boys also, whose bubbling good humour matched Naomi's, but it was she by whom Levi was most impressed. Her intellect, her range of knowledge and her personality left him swimming with admiration and appreciation.

He did remember to steer the conversation occasionally to the rustling. 'We really haven't lost any,' Walt said. 'I keep waiting for it to hit here, but so far it hasn't. Bob Flanagan, the next place east, has lost some, but there hasn't been any of it west of here that I know of at all. Folks over on Ash Creek haven't lost any.'

'That squares with what I've found,' Levi said. 'Sort of bad news, though.'

The whole family looked at him in surprise, waiting for some explanation. He offered it, with a pointed look at Naomi. 'That means I don't have much excuse to hang around over here.'

Laughter broke out around the table. A wave of red swept across Naomi's face, eclipsing momentarily the bridge of freckles across her nose. 'Why should you need an excuse?' she blushed. 'You could come over just because you wanted to.'

'That's the sort of invitation I was wrangling for,' Levi grinned, watching the shade of her blush deepen. 'I just might do that.'

He intended to ride out early the next morning. He waited until he had eaten breakfast with the Hebert family. Then he decided he had time to allow Naomi to show him around the place. He was again impressed with its prosperity. 'Dad likes unusual animals,' Naomi confided, as she showed him some strange, gangly sheep. 'I don't know where he got these sheep, but they have really soft wool.'

She showed him a pair of albino horses, a huge ox that was as tame as a pet dog and a camel. 'I heard tell of them, but I sure ain't never seen one,' Levi admitted.

Naomi smiled. 'He's mean, so be careful. Dad travelled clear to Arizona to buy him and bring him back here.'

'Stinks somethin' terrible, don't he?' Levi asked.

She giggled brightly. He was really sorry when the tour ended and he couldn't find any excuse to stay longer.

Ranch after ranch offered the same report. They had no problem with rustlers. Levi fretted at the waste of time, but he knew it was necessary. He completed the circle of ranches to the west, verifying what Walt Hebert had said. His place was the farthest west the rustling had reached. Mentally he made a map of the places missing cattle, the direction they had gone, and found they almost formed the spokes of a wheel. The hub would lie somewhere north of the place he had lost the trail of the bunch he had followed the night he was shot at.

As he left Ash Creek, he decided it wouldn't be too far out of his way to swing back by the Heberts' place. The closer to Deadhorse Creek he got, the more eager he became to get there. Visions of Naomi's pretty blush nearly caused him to miss the tell-tale cry of disturbed birds in the canyon bottom ahead.

When the sounds registered, he pulled up sharply. Pinpointing the location of the disturbance, he approached it cautiously. Deadhorse Creek meandered a crooked course through a broad valley. Its way was marked by thick stands of cottonwood, interspersed with elm, oak, box elder, hackberry, and occasional walnut trees. In places, the pine timber extended nearly to the hardwood stands. In other places, broad meadows separated them.

Levi followed a neck of timber that jutted out into the valley. Twenty-five yards beyond the end of the timber a huge cottonwood tree stood alone. Beneath that tree a tense group was gathered. Levi sat in the trees straining to listen, but unable to hear. He nudged his horse and approached the group unseen. When he was close enough to hear, he began to put together what was taking place.

'You can't be serious!' a raggedly dressed cowboy was saying. 'I ain't done nothin'!'

'You call this nothin'?' one of the others challenged, holding up a blackened cinch ring.

'What's that got to do with anything?' the first cowboy protested. 'Every cowpoke in Wyoming carries a cinch ring! How else you gonna slap a brand on your outfit's calves that got missed in round-up?'

'How else you gonna run a long rope, you mean,' asserted one of the others. 'Nobody carries them in this country but rustlers. That's evidence enough for me.'

With that he threw his lariat over a branch of the tree. 'Bring him over here boys. Let's get this over with.'

The ragged drifter's pallor deepened to a pasty grey. His voice was plaintive with incredulity. 'You can't just hang me!'

The plea received no hearing. 'We're sick and tired of rustlers in this country,' the first one who spoke, barked.

'You boys get elected judge and jury, did you?' The quiet voice of Levi spun all five heads in his direction. 'I thought this was a civilized country nowadays,' he continued. 'Isn't the usual thing to arrest someone, instead of hanging him?'

'Who are you?' the main speaker of the group demanded.

'Name's Levi Hill,' Levi responded smoothly. 'I'm a range detective. I'm also a deputy sheriff. If you have a complaint against this man, I'll be happy to hear it.'

Relief washed across the captive's face. 'Boy, am I glad to see you! I ain't done nothin'! Honest! I was just ridin' through, lookin' for a job. That's all!'

'We found this in his saddle-bag,' the main speaker of the group broke in belligerently. 'That says 'rustler' as far as I'm concerned.'

'Where you from, son?' Levi asked the terrified cowboy.

'Wyoming,' he gulped. 'I got the idea to work my way back down to Kansas, where my family is, and I need a job for the summer. I ain't stole no cows. Honest, mister!'

'Why don't you just butt out, Deputy,' one of the cowboys who hadn't spoken yet piped up. 'We'll handle this without no help from you.'

'Naw, I guess not,' Levi said easily. 'You boys better just ride. Get back to your outfit. Otherwise, I'll have to arrest you for trying to take the law into your own hands.'

The four immediately began to move their horses to spread out, bracing for a showdown. The captive's face paled again.

Levi swung his horse sideways to the group and brought up a Colt revolving shotgun they hadn't seen before. 'Just sit tight right where you are!' he barked. 'I get real nervous when I'm holding this thing. I can cut all four of you in two before any of you even clear leather.'

They all froze, faces washing clear of colour as though the same solvent poured over each of them. 'Now ease those sidearms out of your holsters and drop them on the ground! Careful!'

They did as he said. 'Now the rifles out of those scabbards!' They complied.

He pointed the shotgun at the closest cowboy to the bound man. 'Now, you, untie that man.'

The designated cowboy nudged his horse beside the captive's and untied his hands. 'Move over here by me,' Levi told him. 'Stay outa my line o' fire, though.'

The man rubbed his wrists a moment, then picked up the reins. He steered his horse in a wide circle, careful not to come between Levi and the rest. 'Now you boys ride out,' Levi ordered. 'I'll drop your guns off at Walt Hebert's. You can pick them up there. You can pass the word that if there's any hanging to do around here, the law will do it. Now ride!'

As they reluctantly started to turn their mounts, Levi fired the shotgun into the air. Their nervous horses jumped, shied, then leaped into a run. When the distance was about right, Levi began firing again, sending buckshot that would only sting into the rumps of the horses. It was all their riders could do to stay in the saddles of the bucking, fleeing, panicked mounts. They were out of sight in minutes.

The newly released captive chuckled in spite of himself. 'Boy, I'm glad you came along!' he said at last. 'I think they really would've hung me!'

'Looked like,' Levi agreed. 'I reckon we'd oughta ride outa here. I doubt they're apt to circle around on us, but they're mad enough they might. One thing about it, their horses aren't going to stand still for them to shoot off of 'em! Shame to make good horses gunshy like that.'

'Am I under arrest?' the drifter asked.

'Nope. Not unless you need to be. A cinch ring ain't used much in this country, but it's no crime to carry one. I'm outa Wyoming myself, so I know everybody packs one.'

'Your name's Hill, huh? I think I heard of you. Was you up around Ten Sleep a few years ago?'

Levi's eyes went flat and hard. He did not answer. 'You ridin' with me, or you headin' for Kansas?'

The rider accepted the change of subject without apparent surprise. 'Well, I sure need a job. I'm plumb outa grub. You know anybody needs a hand?'

Levi pondered it a moment. Finally he said, 'Might. There's a spread over in Antelope Valley, lost a hand a while back. Good outfit, if you're a good worker.'

'I always pull my own weight,' the drifter assured him.

'Well, why don't you ride along with me. We'll be over that way in a day or two.'

The two rode together into Walt Hebert's yard late that afternoon. 'Levi! I didn't expect you back so soon!'

The evident pleasure in Naomi's voice brought a warm rush that spread through Levi like the glow of fine whiskey. 'You don't want to offer a man an invitation unless you expect him to take you up on it,' he responded.

'In that case I'll extend it to you again,' she tossed right back at him.

'Uh, Naomi, this is Bob Winter. Bob, Naomi Hebert.'

Naomi held a hand up and the drifter shook her hand as he would a man's. 'Ma'am. Glad to meet you.'

'Well, both of you, put your horses up and come in. Supper will be ready after a while.'

The drifter proved to be an excellent conversationalist. Levi was glad. It kept the rest of the family busy, allowing him more time to spend with just Naomi.

15

'Are you sure he ain't one of them?'

'Oh, about as sure as I can be, Henry,' Levi replied. 'I got a good look at the tracks of the bunch that stole your heifers, and his horse sure wasn't in that bunch.'

'Are you that good with tracks? To be sure, I mean?'

Levi nodded. 'If I see a track, I'll know it again anywhere I see it. A track is just like a man's face. There ain't no two alike.'

'You think he's OK, do you?' for the fourth time.

'Like I said, he doesn't have any of the signs of ever being on the run or the wrong side of the law. Sleeps like a dead log. He don't jump when a twig breaks out beyond the campfire. He just acts like some farm kid that went to Wyoming to be a cowboy and found out he didn't have a cowboy in him. That's a different world out there. Rough on those that ain't used to it. He's been raised on a farm, though, and I'd guess he'd make you a real hand.'

'Well, I sure do need another hand,' the rancher said, 'what with losin' Robert, and all the delays we've had gettin' the work done. I'll give him a try.'

'You might not want to pay him all he's got comin' till you're ready for him to leave,' Levi offered. 'I'd guess he'll be headin' for Kansas as soon as he gets some money in his pocket again. He's pretty home-sick.'

'Can't fault a man for that,' Henry sympathized. 'He looks like he's fallen on hard times. I asked him about his ma, and I thought he was gonna bawl for just a minute.'

'He thought he wasn't never gonna see her again,' Levi agreed. 'Probably wouldn't have, if I hadn't ridden up at the right time.'

Levi rode out alone the next morning, renewing his rounds of the ranches. At the Clausen ranch he learned Oscar Olson had renewed his efforts to discredit him and have him fired.

The Buchanan ranch had lost another ten head that had been bunched near the road. It was the only bunch of his cows that didn't have a hand staying out of sight to watch them.

'I just didn't have enough hands to watch every bunch,' Chet told him. 'I guess I do now, 'cause I got one bunch less. It was like they knowed just which bunch wasn't bein' watched!'

At the Bertram place, Levi received notice of another meeting of the Cattlemen's Association. It was to be held at the Clausen ranch on Friday afternoon.

On Thursday, Levi spotted tracks he recognized as belonging to one of the rustlers. He had seen the same track with the bunch of Henry's heifers that had been taken. He followed it for nearly three miles before it merged with the other tracks on the road and was lost. 'Half a mile from Olson's place again,' he muttered. 'This is gettin' to be a habit.'

Oscar was still on his mind as he rode into the Clausen yard Friday afternoon. 'Been a long time since I wanted to bust a man as bad as I do him. Every time he opens that mouth of his I just itch to stick a fist in it,' he confided to his horse.

The feeling came back with a vengeance as he walked into the meeting. The strident voice of Oscar Olson met him half way through the door. 'So you really started showin' your true colours! What do you have to say for yourself? It's bad enough that you save an obvious member of the rustlers' gang from the hanging he deserves, but you don't even arrest him! You get him a job!'

Levi glanced around the room. There were more openly hostile faces than he had faced before. Henry's face was red and the blood vessels at his temple pulsed visibly. Faces that had been neutral toward him showed either caution or animosity. Few faces were at all sympathetic. He turned his attention to Olson.

'Since when is riding through the country evidence of being part of a gang of rustlers?' he asked quietly.

'Since he had a cinch ring in his saddle-bag, that's since when. A cinch ring that was blackened by a good many branding fires! Why else would he have it, if he wasn't changing brands?' Olson demanded.

'What makes you think any brands have been changed?' Levi reasoned. 'We haven't found a shred of evidence the stolen cattle are having their brands changed. If they were, it wouldn't be by a lone rustler riding alone. He's no rustler.'

'I say he is,' Olson roared. 'I say he is and you deliberately kept him here. I say you're part of it!'

Levi fought the rising tide of his anger. He started to answer Olson, but was interrupted by another rancher. 'Hill, I ain't that quick to accuse,' Gill McDougal said, 'but I'd sure like to know why you're so sure he ain't part of the rustlers.'

Levi looked around again at the ring of belligerent faces. He turned back to Olson. His stomach tightened as he saw that Olson had drawn his gun while his attention was diverted and held it inches away from Levi's stomach.

'Badge or no badge, Hill,' Olson shouted, 'you're under arrest. I'm accusing you of being a rustler and a friend to rustlers. I'm taking you to town to lock you up and if you try something before we get there I'll shed no tears!'

There was a collective gasp, then a deathly silence descended on the room.

'Put it away, Oscar,' Levi said, in a voice that bore quiet whispers of death. 'I don't want to have to kill you.'

'Don't give me that big talk!' Olson jabbed him in the stomach with the gun barrel. 'Just get your hands up!'

Nobody really saw what happened. Levi simply swept Oscar's gun aside as his fist crashed into the man's chin. Olson's gun fired harmlessly into the wall beside Levi and the man crumpled into a heap. Levi quickly scanned the faces around him for further danger. Nobody had seen him draw his gun, but it was in his hand. He holstered it, stooped to pick up the fallen rancher's weapon and handed it to Clausen.

'Give it back to him when you think he's got sense enough to pack one.'

'How'd you do that?' a faceless voice in the crowd asked.

Levi just shrugged. 'Doesn't matter. The man's all mouth. Somebody's going to shut it for him one of these times. I hope they just whip him good. I'd hate to see a man get killed just because he has a big mouth.'

'How sure are you the guy you took to Hawkinson's ain't one of the rustlers?'

Levi studied the continuing distrust

in the man's face. 'About as sure as I can be, I guess. He sure ain't one that was along when they took Henry's heifers. He don't carry any of the signs of a man that's ever been on the wrong side of the law. If he's stole any cows he ain't got any of the money from 'em, and he ain't spent any buyin' clothes. I guess I'm as sure of him as I am of Walt Hebert there.'

'Yeah, we heard you found out Walt's got a daughter,' someone said.

Two or three laughed, but the look on Levi's face caused it to halt in mid-breath. A lane suddenly opened between Levi and the speaker as men crowded back out of the line. Levi's eyes bored into the suddenly serious face of Al Holt, the youngest rancher in the bunch. 'No offence!' the man said hurriedly.

Whatever Levi was about to say was lost as another rancher entered the room. Casey Malone strode purposefully into the room, then stopped suddenly on seeing Olson's prone form on the floor. 'What happened to Oscar?' he demanded.

'He went and pulled a gun on Hill,' Henry answered.

'He dead? You kill 'im?' he asked of Levi.

Levi shook his head. 'Naw, I just tried to tap a little sense into him. He'll come around pretty quick.'

'Well I'm not surprised he's been raising so much fuss,' Casey asserted. 'I've been over to Hay Springs and I found out something the rest of you should know.'

The room fell silent again. He hooked his thumb in the front of his pants as he continued, 'The banker over at Hay Springs is my wife's cousin by marriage. She was a Dawkins, you know. We was over there yesterday and I just happened to mention something about this whole situation over here. He told me something that might shed a lot of light on what's going on.'

He looked around the room, obviously enjoying the spotlight of the assembly's attention. 'It seems that Oscar Olson banks over there. It seems that Oscar Olson borrowed a lot of money. He couldn't pay it back and the bank was getting ready to foreclose on his ranch. Then one day he comes in and says he sold a bunch of cattle so he could pay his mortgage. Paid off the whole thing, he did.'

'What?'

'The whole thing?'

'How could he do that?'

'Where'd he get that kinda money?'

'When was that, Casey?'

'Now, there you've asked the right question.' Casey held up a finger like a lecturing professor. 'When was that? That was after Oscar Olson was complaining about the rustlers stealing so many of his cattle and saying that's why he was having money problems. That was less than six months after the rustling began!'

'Well, he'd sure know what herds was bein' watched,' someone said.

'Know! He's the one that decided

which bunches ought to have a guard and which ones probably didn't need one!'

'Yeah, and it was always a bunch he said didn't need one that got stole!'

Casey looked like a hellfire-and-brimstone preacher. His red hair bushed out from his balding head. The stark white of his scalp above the line where his hat brim rode, made him look like the top of his head was lit from within. He began to stroke his audience like a fiddler tuning his instrument.

'All this time we've been trying to figure out what to do about these rustlers before we brought in a detective, who was directing the whole show?'

'Oscar!'

'Who's been trying the hardest to get rid of the range detective?'

'Olson!'

'Who has been accusing everybody that comes his way of being one of the rustlers to divert suspicion away from himself?'

'Olson!'

'Who is the most logical to lie in wait for that Blundell boy and shoot him in cold blood?'

'Olson!'

He had them! He had them in the palm of his hand. He had practised this speech in his mind all the way from Hay Springs and they were responding exactly as he knew they must. The heady feeling of being in control robbed him of all reason.

'Who needs to be taken out in the yard and hanged from the closest tree?' he yelled, waiting for the cries of 'Olson' to reach a deadly crescendo.

The response was all wrong. He was toppled from his heady perch where he held the reins of the assembled humanity. Instead of the unstoppable conclusion that would carry Oscar to his death, the wrong voice responded. 'Not this day!'

Attention jumped to Levi. 'Not this day or any other day that I wear a badge!' he barked. 'This is a country of law and order, not mob rule. If Olson is guilty, I'll take a special measure of pride and a real personal pleasure in taking him in. But all we have right now is a bunch of what's called circumstantial evidence. I'll not stand for a man being hanged on circumstantial evidence. I'll sure not stand for a man bein' lynched by a bunch of mad cowmen.'

The crowd looked from Levi to Casey and back again. Casey looked crestfallen.

'But he's guilty!' he insisted.

Olson groaned and started to stir. The circle of men drew back so that Levi, Casey and Olson were in the same circle. Nobody said a word for the full time it took Oscar to regain consciousness. He struggled to his feet, holding his chin and head, trying to clear his vision.

When he had time to clear his head, Levi spoke. 'Oscar, we've just learned you came by a sizeable chunk of money shortly after the rustling started. Enough to pay off your note at the bank. You want to tell us where you got that money?'

'I don't want to tell you the time of day,' the surly rancher growled. 'Not you or anyone else. My business is my business. What's the matter with all you men? You stand around like ninnies and let this man gun-whip me, then let him start asking me questions? What's going on here?'

'He didn't gun-whip you, Oscar. He's got a punch like gettin' kicked by a bay steer, though.'

'Where'd you get the money, Oscar?' someone called. 'You're quick enough to accuse everyone else. Answer for yourself!'

'I don't have to answer to any of you!' Olson yelled, regaining some of his lost volume. 'If you don't want my help, find your own rustlers. But I'm tellin' you, you ain't going to, as long as you keep that rustler-lovin' lawman around.'

He grabbed his hat and started for

the door. A couple of ranchers moved to block his way, but Levi spoke. 'Let him go. We don't have cause to hold him. Yet.'

The cattlemen did, slowly and reluctantly. They were in a state of confusion. There were still some that openly questioned Levi, but the intervention and quiet arguments of Walt Hebert pretty well restored a tentative faith in him. One by one the ranchers drifted away. When it was obvious nothing more was going to be revealed, solved, or drawn to a conclusion, Levi also left.

16

The rising sun reflected red off a line of clouds that covered the western horizon. 'Going to rain,' Levi told his horse. 'That means a bunch of cattle's going to move today or tonight, sure's anything. Let's head back over to King Canyon. That's the way everything moves. Maybe we'll get lucky and spot something on the way by.'

He set out at a steady trot. Nightfall found him most of the way to his goal. The wind had picked up from the south, even though the clouds were coming in from the west. The edge of the front was led by towering thunderheads. By dark, sharp lightning was flashing intermittently.

Lightning increased as the storms approached. A tall pine, about 300 yards from Levi and his horse, split from top to bottom with an ear-splitting crack. The entire tree was bathed in a ball of fire. Thunder deafened them. The horse quivered between his knees. The stricken tree burst into flame. Only the immediate beginning of the rain kept it from sparking the whole area into an inferno of burning timber.

The rain began at once, and in earnest. It came in sheets, driving its cold through man and animal. It blew through the cracks and gaps in Levi's slicker, soaking him to the skin. Wind and water plastered his hat brim down against his face. He finally spotted a cutbank that offered some shelter, and dismounted. Man and horse huddled against the lee of the bank. Blinded and deafened by the constant crack and roar of lightning and thunder, they could do nothing but cower together and wait for the onslaught to end.

It ended as quickly as it had begun. The thundering wall of lightning and water marched away to the east; leaving a soft rain in its wake. The world seemed suddenly almost surrealistically serene. Levi mounted up again.

'C'mon Champ. Let's go see what we can find.'

Within three miles dust kicked from beneath the horse's hooves. 'Pretty spotty rain,' he commented with enthusiasm at the unexpected advantage. 'Maybe we'll get lucky tonight yet. Just might run across some tracks that didn't wash out.'

Less than a mile later he did. He was barely able to see the road itself in the dark, so it was a real stroke of luck that he spotted the small chokecherry bush that had been trampled beside the road. He dismounted and struck a match, cupping it against the wind.

'Whatd'ya know!' he whispered. 'Just what we've been looking for!'

He stood in the road pondering for several minutes. 'If I go blundering on down the road, I'll ride right on past any sign I need to see. On the other hand, it looks like the worst of the storm is past. Might be there won't come enough rain to wipe out any more tracks. I'd best wait till daylight, then see where these lead.'

He knew he never could have followed sign from where the cattle had been stolen. The furious thunderstorms would surely have obliterated those tracks, most places, but there was a good chance of being able to follow them from here.

He rode away from the road, back up into the timber. He staked out his horse on a patch of good, rain-washed grass, and rolled into his bedroll without a fire and without supper.

He was in the saddle again at first light. It had rained again in the night but not heavily enough to wipe away all sign, if he was lucky. He returned to the trampled bush. 'Not much sign left,' he lamented. 'Looks like they came from over east, and moved 'em on to this road, just like before. Well let's see if I can find where they leave the road again.'

He rode slowly along, watching carefully for any sign. Several wagons passed him in either direction. Riders in ones, twos, and threes went by. A couple of hands from Bertram's ranch came by, driving a dozen head of yearling heifers. 'Regular highway,' he muttered.

He rode down into King Canyon itself. The road had too much traffic to distinguish the tracks of the dozen or so cows he was trying to track, especially after being fairly well washed out by the spotty rain. He contented himself to scour both sides of the road for any sign of their leaving it.

At the bottom of the canyon, the road became narrow, fenced off on both sides by brush. He crossed washes, where those driving wagons had to fill the ditches the rain washed across the road. He climbed the hill back into timber as the road left the canyon for a brief way. As he started back down into the canyon further north, he still had not found any exit marks of the stolen cattle. He crossed another low swale, and rode about a hundred yards beyond. He pulled his horse to a stop, dismounted and walked across the road and back twice. 'Maybe I'm nuts,' he said aloud, 'but it looks like less tracks than there were back a ways.'

He turned around and rode back the way he had come. Beyond the wash the traces of tracks were, in fact, thicker. He doubled back once again, watching the road intently. He thought he saw a familiar horse's hoof mark in the road and bent to look at it more closely. As he bent forward his hat flew from his head.

The sound of the rifle reached him as he was already in the air on the way to the ground. He rolled into a chokecherry bush, drew his gun, and waited. Now what happened to all that traffic? he asked himself silently. There ain't a soul in sight.

He waited several minutes, watching his horse. The animal had been intent on something in the direction from which the shot had come. His ears were forward. His muscles were tense.

He was standing at attention. Now his ears began to twitch as flies buzzed around him, and he began to pay more attention to them than what he had been looking at or listening to. 'Sure hope you ain't lying to me,' Levi muttered at the horse.

He circled carefully around the chokecherry bush without drawing any fire. Finally he walked back into the open. Nothing happened. He followed the edge of the road down into the large wash. He turned up the wash, following it at right angles from the road. Twenty feet from the edge of the road he stopped.

'Brush marks!' he breathed. 'Wasn't enough rain this time! Some of the tracks didn't wash out, so somebody tried to brush 'em out. Looks like we finally found what we're looking for!'

He retrieved his hat, clamping his jaw as he pushed his finger through the bullet hole in its crown. Mounting, he rode back south-east a quartermile, then turned off the road heading in the same direction the wash led. 'If you think I'm going to ride up the bottom of that draw to follow you, you're nuts!' he gritted.

He followed the ridge, riding slowly and carefully. He scanned the area every time he emerged from the timber. He stayed far enough down from the top of the ridge to avoid silhouetting himself against the sky. He followed the winding of the wide wash as it turned up connecting canyons, leading always eastward.

His stomach was a tight knot in his middle. The hair on the back of his neck prickled every time he rode across an open space. He had the distinct feeling he was either going to learn something or meet a sudden death. He was not at all sure which, but the premonition grew as he rode.

He was more than two miles from the road when he drew up sharply. At the edge of the canyon directly below him, a large corral was concealed in a huge grove of hardwood. He studied it with appreciation. 'There ain't three places you could even see the corral from,' he breathed admiringly. 'Even if someone did figure out how they left the road, they'd likely ride right on past without even seeing it.'

He pondered his next move. If he accosted them now, he could probably arrest the ones who were with the cattle. If he waited and watched, he could find out where they moved them from here, how they dispensed with them, and who the mastermind of the operation was. He decided on the latter.

He found a relatively flat spot, well hidden from all sides, and staked out his horse. He exchanged his boots for a pair of moccasins from his saddle-bags, and slipped down the hill. He counted about sixty head of cattle in the corral. No hay and no water, so they ain't going to keep 'em long, he told himself silently.

He worked a complete circle around the holding area. He counted five men killing time around a small smokeless fire. A coffee pot sat on the edges of its coals. As he watched, the men rolled into their blankets and began to sleep.

Good idea, he reflected. Nobody's going to move before dark.

He returned to his horse. He breakfasted on dry biscuits, venison jerky, and water from his canteen. Then he, too, rolled into his blankets in a patch of thick brush. He tried his best to sleep, but he could not. That knot of premonition in his stomach offered him no rest.

17

By dark, Levi was packed up and his horse was saddled. Two more men rode into the rustlers' camp. He heard hushed conversations, then the cattle were moved quietly out of the corral. Good hands with stock, he admired, noting the minimum of noise made in getting the cattle moving.

As they moved back down the wide wash, they stopped at every large mud hole, draining it of its contents. By the time they reached the road the cattle were no longer thirsty. As they strung them out on the road, one man said, 'Keep 'em moving. Mary 'n me'll brush out the tracks.'

Levi waited until the two had come back to rejoin their fellows, then he moved off into the night, following their sound. 'I'll just have to trust your ears, Champ,' he told the horse

176

he was already learning to appreciate. Mattie had given him Robert's horse when his own was worn down with the constant riding. 'You sure better tell me if there's someone waiting for me.'

Three hours later the moon came up. It was only a quarter moon, but it offered enough light to make travel on the road easier. When the riders turned the cattle off the main road on to a smaller one leading west, the same two fell back to brush out the tracks. They cut large clumps of brush and wiped away all traces of the cattle for almost half a mile, taking over an hour to do so. They carried their makeshift brooms with them, dropping them in a dry gulch nearly a mile beyond.

The sky was lightening in the east when they turned off that road into a broad shallow canyon. A small creek ran along one edge. The broad bottom was lush with grass. The cattle moved without direction to the creek to drink, then spread out on the grass, eating hungrily.

The men gathered at the upper end of the canyon in a grove of cottonwood trees, and unsaddled their horses. 'Looks like another stop for the day,' Levi muttered. 'They got this whole thing planned out pretty well.'

As darkness approached, they were all up again. The rustlers gathered the cattle together, while Levi watched from his hidden vantage point. They moved out, heading due north. Three hours later they crossed the White River, still moving north. Two hours beyond that, the newly risen moon revealed a cluster of corrals, a water tower, and a depot. 'Dakota Junction!' Levi breathed. 'They drive 'em clear up here to Dakota Junction, and ship 'em on the railroad! No wonder we couldn't find what they were doing with them!'

He moved as close as he dared without risking discovery. He saw the seven rustlers gather together, then a man separated himself from the shadows of the depot. 'How many this time, men?' he asked. The voice struck a bell in Levi's memory, but he couldn't place it.

'Fifty-eight,' the biggest of the rustlers replied. Levi had recognized him from the fight at the Ash Creek dance. He had recognized four of them in all, but three were still unknown to him, besides the one who was obviously the mastermind. Money was silently counted and parcelled out to the men.

'Whatever you can get in the next thirty days,' he instructed, 'have up here the last of the month. My buyer will be here again the first.'

'That range detective was nosin' around the canyon a few nights ago. Right after we brung in the last bunch. I think he figured out where we take 'em up that draw.'

'What! He found it?'

Levi saw the big man's teeth flash in the moonlight. 'Yeah, but don't worry about it. He ain't no more problem.

I put a little round piece of daylight through his thick skull and left him lying there in the road.'

'You shot him?'

'Yup.'

'You sure you got him?'

'Dropped like a poleaxed steer,' the man said with conviction. 'I don't know who found 'im, but he was gone when we came out with the cows.'

The boss nodded silently and turned on his heel. Levi could get a general idea of his size and build, but could see nothing more. He fingered his gun speculatively. Counting up the odds, he left it where it was. He stood without moving until all of them had ridden away, and the night had fallen silent except for the tired shuffling of the cattle.

When he was sure everyone was gone, he walked to where the man in charge had stood. Cupping a match in his hands, he stooped and looked at the tracks.

'Same man,' he muttered. 'You and me are gonna meet one of these days.'

He mounted his horse and rode out, heading for Chadron. He considered renting one of the fancy rooms at the brand new Blaine Hotel. Remembering the rustlers thought he was dead, he thought better of it. Instead he found a secluded spot south of town where a small spring was hidden in a little vale and camped.

He spent some time with the sheriff, sharing information and making plans. The sheriff agreed they should do nothing until they were able to identify the rest of the rustlers, and especially the one masterminding the operation.

'Why don't you get word to the Cattlemen's Association to meet at Buchanan's day after tomorrow,' Levi suggested.

'You'll be there?'

'I'll be there.'

'They're going to push pretty hard to do something against the ones you've identified.'

'I don't intend to identify anybody to them.'

'Even the ones you recognized?'

'Nope. If I hang a tag on anyone, the first cowboy that sees him will shoot him. Or try to. I'd just as soon they didn't know that their identities were known.'

'You going to let them keep on thinking you're dead?'

'As long as I can. You might have someone spread a rumour to that effect. I'll try to stay out of sight. Can you chase down the buyer that's dealing with the rustlers?'

'Shouldn't be too hard.'

'Will he help you hang on to the cattle without tipping anyone off?'

'He will if he don't want to be hanged for being in with the rustlers.'

They made a few other plans and Levi left. He rode out at dark, riding all night. He reached Hebert's place along Deadhorse Creek shortly after sun-up.

Naomi flew from the house to meet him. 'Levi! Oh, I'm so glad to see you!

They told me you were dead! They said you had been shot.'

She flung herself into his arms and he held her tightly for as long as he thought her joyous surprise would allow him to do so. When he released her, she stepped back, but she kept a hand on his arm. It felt warm and exciting just resting there.

Levi grinned, his sagging spirits and tired body buoyed by the obvious delight of the very pretty woman. 'Naw. I'm about half shot, though. You reckon I could rest awhile?'

She took his hands again and looked him over carefully. Her eyes shone. 'Oh, I was so, so, oh, I'm just so glad you're OK. Your hat! You did get shot at!'

He took his hat off and grinned ruefully at it. 'Don't keep the rain out worth a darn, now,' he lamented.

Just then Walt Hebert walked around the corner of the house. He was carrying a bucket nearly full of warm milk. As he rounded the corner of the house he spotted Levi. He stopped abruptly. His jaw dropped. The bucket fell from his suddenly limp fingers. It hit the ground and tipped over, spilling its warm foamy contents all over the bright blossoms of his wife's flower bed.

'Levi!' he breathed incredulously. 'I thought you was dead!'

'Came close,' Levi admitted. 'Got lucky again.'

Hebert quickly recovered his composure. 'Well, now look what I did! I was so surprised to see you standing on two feet I went and dropped the milk.'

'Isn't this just a wonderful surprise?' Naomi enthused.

'Well yes! The best! I didn't know what we were going to do for an investigator,' Walt agreed. With a twinkle returning to his eyes he added, 'I'm sure that was Naomi's biggest concern, too.'

Naomi blushed and turned back to Levi. 'Put your horse up and come on in.'

'Thanks, I will. Oh, I'd just as soon

that nobody except the Association knows I'm still alive. The rustlers might get careless if they think I'm out of the picture.'

Naomi nodded silently. Walt looked thoughtful as he also nodded his assent.

Levi felt a great deal better when he left the next day to attend the meeting.

18

It was a study in contrasts to watch the expressions on those entering the room of the meeting. Levi arrived early. He stationed himself where the ranchers would see him as they walked in. Some registered shock; some looked relieved, some gave no indication it wasn't the most natural thing in the world for him to be there.

Henry was one of the latter. 'You didn't seem surprised to see me,' Levi commented, as they awaited the arrival of the late-comers.

'Why would I be?' Henry answered. 'I figured you were the one that called the meeting.'

'You hadn't heard I was dead?'

'No. Were you?'

Caught off guard, Levi exploded in laughter. When he recovered his composure he showed his friend his hat. 'Well, now, that's a novel idea,' Henry said dryly. 'Does that let out the heat pretty good on a hot day?'

'Gives a vent both ways,' Levi responded, with his face just as straight and serious. 'It also keeps it from gettin' blowed off by the hot air when I'm around certain people.'

Henry grinned in response. 'Somebody took another shot at you, huh?'

Levi nodded. 'Word seems to have gotten around that I was dead, too. Walt Hebert plumb dropped a fresh bucket of milk when he saw me. Spilled it all over his wife's flowers.'

'I bet he caught it for that!' Henry observed. 'She puts a lot of stock in those flowers.'

'Whole family puts a lot of stock in the looks of the place,' Levi agreed. 'I never did see a place fixed up that nice. All built with saw-milled lumber. Real siding on the house, just like in town. They even got the barn and stuff painted.'

Henry agreed. 'I always wondered

how he could afford all that,' he said. 'He must be a mighty good manager of money. Place ain't big enough to support that much fixin' up otherwise.'

'How much stock does he run?'

'I don't know, exactly. Don't think he could have a hundred head, though. Don't farm, except hay. Sure does well though.'

'I figured the place was bigger than that,' Levi said. 'With two sons nearly grown and a full-time hand, he could run a lot bigger place than that, seems like.'

They were interrupted by the arrival of the missing members of the Association. Oscar Olson blustered in with the last ones, chin jutted forward belligerently even as he walked through the door. Upon seeing Levi he stopped dead in his tracks.

'Hill!' he said, too loudly. 'I heard you was killed! I thought we was rid of you. I don't care who knows I'm sorry to see it ain't true.'

'It's good to see you too, Oscar,' Levi

replied. His face smiled at Oscar, but his eyes were like pieces of blue fire.

'I bet you hoped he was dead,' Casey Malone said. 'Levi, you best tell us what we're here for, before I smash that stupid Swede's mouth.' Malone turned to Oscar as an afterthought. 'And if you butt in one time while he's talkin', I will!'

Levi took a step forward and raised his voice to take command, before things got out of hand. 'I asked for this meeting because I have learned some things. I found where the cattle are being held, where they're taken and how they're gotten out of the country.'

Oscar Olson had been glaring at Casey Malone. As Levi said that, his head snapped around to face him, and his jaw began working spasmodically. 'You know who's doin' it?' he asked, his face paling noticeably.

The change in his demeanour was not lost on the assembled ranchers. Several looked at each other meaningfully.

'Some of them,' Levi answered. 'I'll start at the beginning, and fill you in.'

He told them the story. 'I recognized four of the men. I have a good picture of the other three in my head. I'll know them when I see them.'

'How about the boss?' somebody asked.

'I'm not sure,' Levi said.

Casey Malone nodded to a rancher standing beside Oscar Olson. At his nod the man reached out and pulled Oscar's gun from his holster.

'Hey!' Oscar howled. 'What do you think you're doing?'

'We're asking you some questions, Oscar,' Casey said. 'And you know why we're asking. Here you are, just about to lose your place to the bank. Then the rustling starts and you keep crying about how many cows you're losing. Then you just happen to pay off everything you owe at the bank.'

'I told you that money is none of your business!' Olson shouted.

Malone held up his hand. 'Have it your way. Then this Texas horse trader comes along and you try your best to make everyone think he's a horsethief and a rustler. Then he says we should get a range detective and you were the only one who didn't want one brought in.'

Oscar made a valiant effort to maintain his bluster. 'Well, I didn't. We don't need some outsider trying to settle our problems,' he fumed.

Malone lifted his hand for silence again. 'Then when we hire one anyway, you do everything you can to make us all think that he's somehow in cahoots with the rustlers. But all this time you are the one who knows just what bunch of cattle can be stolen, and when, without getting caught.'

'That's ridiculous,' Olson said, his face getting pastier by the minute.

'Now, when you see Hill, here, you look like you seen a ghost. Then when you hear that he knows who some of the rustlers are and where they take the cattle, Oscar, you looked like you was going to get sick to your stomach. I guess we already know who the boss of the rustlin' is. It's you, Oscar!'

Oscar's mouth worked frantically, but no sound came out. He swallowed noisily and tried again, to no avail. 'We talked long enough,' Jack Bertram said. 'Much as I hate to think it, I got no choice. Hill, I reckon you better arrest Oscar.'

'Hang him!' somebody shouted.

A chorus of agreement rang out at once, and the group started to move toward Oscar. He cowered backward, hands held up in front of him, as though to ward off their charges. 'Wait a minute!' Levi barked. 'There ain't going to be any hanging! Now everybody move back and listen!'

Reluctantly the group fell back. Levi pushed Oscar toward the wall, and stationed himself where he could prevent anyone from trying to grab him. 'I ain't sure who the rest of the outfit are, or who's running the outfit, but I have a plan to find out. Four of the rustlers I know, and I've given the sheriff their names. I've given him a description of three others. I will soon know the rest. When I have the evidence to prove it, I'll arrest the guilty.'

'You going to take them on alone?' someone called.

'I got a better question,' Casey Malone bristled. 'You going to take all of us on alone, to keep us from hangin' that thievin' Olson right now?'

'If I have to, yes, I will,' Levi said, a new quiet edge to his voice.

'I don't reckon you have to,' Henry said. He stepped over beside Levi, further shielding Oscar from the rest of the men.

Immediately, Walt Hebert did the same. With obvious reluctance, two more ranchers stepped across to offer their support as well.

'I'm convinced Oscar's guilty as sin,' Chet Buchanan said, 'but I ain't gonna live with knowin' we hung a man without bein' sure, or lettin' the law do it.'

Casey looked around at the others. Failing to see the support he needed, he backed off.

'We'll be goin' now,' Levi said, that quiet edge still on his voice.

The five men made a circle around Oscar and pushed him toward the door. They continued to shield him all the way to their horses. They mounted, riding out of the yard. When they were well clear of the yard, Levi pulled up. 'Oscar,' he said, addressing the subdued rancher, 'I'll be askin' you to stay close to home and stay out of sight. If any of your neighbours see you away from home, I can't guarantee your safety.'

'You lettin' him go?' Chet asked incredulously.

'Ain't got enough evidence to hold him,' Levi conceded reluctantly.

Without waiting for any further conversation, Oscar kicked his horse harshly. He started up the road at a gallop. The five sat their horses, watching him go.

'Henry, I'd like for you to ride with me for a ways,' Levi said finally.

Recognizing there was nothing left they were required for, the other three mumbled goodbyes and rode off. When they were clear of earshot, Levi addressed his friend. 'Henry, I'd like for you to round up ten men you're real sure you can trust. I'd like to have Homer among 'em, 'cause I know he's mighty handy with a gun and he's got good sense. We need eight or ten like that. Meet me at Dakota Junction as soon as you can.'

Henry's eyebrows shot up. 'Dakota Junction, huh? Where you going to be?'

'I got to talk to the sheriff. Then I'll scout around Dakota Junction a while. I'll have a spot picked out by the time you get there.'

'You'll meet us?'

'I'll meet you well south of there. If I ain't there, wait till I get there. I don't want all your tracks where they'll see 'em when they ride in next time.'

When Henry had ridden away, Levi rode as quickly as he could to town. He and the sheriff talked at length. Levi shared the other evidence implicating Oscar. 'I'm almost sure he ain't the brains of it,' he concluded, 'but it's plumb certain he's involved some way.'

'You reckon they'll wait till the end of the month to grab the next bunch?' the sheriff asked.

Levi's answer demonstrated that he had already thought that question through. He said, 'Not likely.'

The sheriff's eyebrows lifted. 'Why not?'

'It's not likely what went on at the meeting tonight will stay quiet,' Levi reasoned. 'Somebody's sure to go home and tell his wife, she'll tell someone else. It'll be all over the country by tomorrow. I'd thought to keep it quiet that they hadn't killed me, but I had to go to that meeting and everyone'll know now.'

'What makes you so sure the one runnin' the rustlers ain't one of them ranchers?' the sheriff asked.

'I been watchin' tracks,' Levi explained. 'Every meeting I look the yard over. I've seen a lot of that man's boot tracks. I'd know 'em in a fruit cellar without a lantern if I had a blindfold on. Them boots ain't been to a one of them meetings. That's why I'm sure it ain't Oscar.'

'You think they'll just back off and quit takin' cows?' the sheriff offered.

'Maybe. I'd guess it's more likely they'd make one last big drive. They know I gave you the names of four of them and descriptions of the other three. They got to leave the country, but I'd guess they'll try to make one more drive first.'

'So what have you got planned to do?' he asked.

Levi ignored the question for the moment. 'Did you find the buyer?' he asked.

The sheriff smiled ruefully. 'I found

him. He's got the last bunch held at the stockyards down by the railroad track here in town.'

'How'd he pay for them?'

'Cash.'

'Did he admit to knowin' they was stolen?'

'Naw, 'course not,' the sheriff scoffed. 'He's just about as innocent a man as you ever saw in your life. He says the guy told him he was travelling around, buying bunches of cows here and there that the ranchers wanted to get rid of. Claimed the guy had bills-of-sale for all of them.'

'He give you a name?'

'He said the guy called himself George Winslow.'

'We'll have to have him take a look at Oscar first chance we get. See if he's George Winslow. I'd bet you this month's wages he ain't, though.'

'I thought I'd do that,' the sheriff agreed.

Levi returned to the sheriff's question. 'I asked Henry to round up about ten men he's real sure we can trust, and meet me at Dakota Junction as soon as he can get them there. I told him to have them bring along some grub. We'll just sort of camp out of sight up there, and see what shows up in the next couple of days.'

'Watch yourself,' the sheriff warned. 'I won't hold still for no turkey shoot.'

'I never killed a man I didn't have to yet,' Levi assured him.

The sheriff studied him a long moment, then nodded.

19

After his visit with the sheriff, Levi rode directly to Dakota Junction. He sat his horse a quarter-mile away, watching the train station. A train was stopped there, waiting for the railroader to throw the switch to turn the train on to the northbound track. He signalled the engineer and the train began to huff and puff, emitting huge clouds of steam. It moved slowly until the last car was beyond the switch. The switchman threw the switch back again, waved a signal to the engineer, and swung aboard. The train huffed off to the north, gathering speed toward South Dakota.

Levi rode a long circle around the entire area. He settled finally on a shallow ravine almost a half-mile north of the corrals. Several large trees clustered around a trickle of water. The area was well hidden from the corrals. Even from the roof of the depot it would be impossible to see anyone in the ravine.

I wonder why they put a depot there? he asked himself suddenly. They sure didn't think another town'd start up here, this close to Chadron, did they?

The question drifted off in the hot breeze. Late the next afternoon he saw small puffs of dust to the south. He mounted and rode a wide circle, hoping it was Henry and the men. As he drew closer he recognized his friend and several others. They spotted him and veered their course to approach his position.

'You made good time, Henry,' Levi called.

'Looks like you guessed right,' Henry called back.

Levi did not respond. He waited as the group approached and stopped. As the dust settled, Henry explained. 'They's bunches of cattle missing all over! I'd guess there's fifty or sixty head that'll be on the way here in a day or two.'

'Not waitin' for rain anymore, huh?'

'Not waitin' for nothin'. Looks like they're just tryin' to grab as many as they can, as fast as they can.'

'Well, let's hope they keep the same pattern, and bring 'em here,' Levi worried.

They camped in the ravine for two boiling days. They kept two men on watch at all times. Levi gave strict orders to have no smoking and no fire during daylight, even to cook food. That meant no coffee, except after dark and before daylight.

'One wisp of smoke somebody can spot is all we need to blow up the whole deal,' he said.

'You think someone'll be watching the junction?' Henry asked, surprise evident in his voice.

'I'll be surprised if he doesn't,' Levi said. 'This guy has been pretty slick, up to now. I doubt he's going to get dumb and careless that sudden.'

'You still don't think it's Oscar?'

Levi didn't answer for a long while. Finally he said, 'No. I think he's involved, but Oscar's all mouth and no brain. Whoever the boss of this outfit is, he's smart.'

It was two hours before daylight of the third day when the lookout woke the sleeping group. 'Sounds like activity, way off south,' he said.

The rest sprang from their bedrolls, listening. Faintly on the breeze they could hear cattle bawling, and an occasional subdued yell of a cowboy. 'Grab your guns and take the positions I showed you,' Levi said tersely. 'Remember, I want nobody shot unless they start shooting first. And I don't want our presence given away, if we can help it, till the boss gets there.'

They scurried around, grabbing their things and running on foot to take up the stations Levi had assigned to each. They were in place for the better part of an hour before the cattle arrived.

One man rode at a lope to open the

huge double gates of the main corral. He rode beneath the long pole that braced the gate and made a complete circle of the corral, then rode back out at a lope.

Within minutes the cattle began streaming in. They were dusty and tired. Tongues lolled out the sides of their mouths. Their sides were streaked with sweat. As soon as they were all in, two riders shut the gates. 'Well there they are, boys,' the huge leader Levi recognized as Joe Broderick said. 'Now all we gotta do is wait for the boss to show up, get our money, and light outa this country.'

'I'd like to have me a stab at that lawman first,' one whose voice Levi recognized as Luke Walker said.

'Forget him,' the big man rapped. 'He'd chew you up and spit you out like a chokecherry seed.'

'What was that?' a third rustler said.

The rustlers all grabbed for their guns. 'What'd you hear?' Joe asked.

'I ain't sure,' the other replied.

'Sounded like a spur hit a fence post. There's somebody here!'

Levi knew he dared wait no longer. 'Throw down your guns, boys! You're surrounded.'

Guns barked and fire stabbed toward the sound of Levi's voice. In response a fusillade exploded from the waiting cowboys. Horses squealed and reared, men were falling, cursing, and yelling. The scene turned from calm to wild pandemonium in seconds. 'Hold your fire!' Levi yelled, then ducked to one side in case they shot at his voice again.

'Don't shoot! Don't shoot!' one of the rustlers was screaming. 'I'm hit! I give up! Don't shoot!'

'All of you, drop your guns!' Levi barked.

'They're dropped! They're dropped!' several voices called at once.

'Get your hands up high, and walk out in the open,' Levi instructed.

Four men marched out, almost running, into the open moonlight.

'Where's the others?' Levi demanded.

'They're down,' one of the four declared.

'Watch 'em boys,' Levi said.

He slipped out from behind the corner of the depot, moving quickly. He stepped up where he could see the three downed outlaws on the ground. Only one of them was moving. He was trying to drag himself toward the shelter of the corral fence.

'Stop right where you are,' Levi ordered.

The man stopped and looked around at Levi. 'I need help,' he said, weakly.

Levi approached warily. He could not see the man's right hand, the way he was lying on the ground. One leg jutted out at an impossible angle, but he appeared otherwise unhurt.

'Get your other hand out here where I can see it,' he commanded.

'Sure, sure,' the man complied.

As his hand came into sight the moon reflected off metal. Levi fired at almost the same time the rustler did. He felt the angry buzz of the bullet past his head and saw the outlaw jerk spasmodically. He fired again. The man collapsed, unmoving.

Levi walked over and turned him over with his toe. He was dead. He quickly checked the other two. They were dead as well. The big man's shirt was so filled with holes it looked like moths had eaten it.

He walked back to the others. His own men had formed a line facing the captured criminals. 'Put them on their horses,' Levi commanded curtly.

Several of them looked at Levi in surprise, but they did as he said. 'Tie their hands behind them,' he said.

Looking at each other again, they did so. Levi walked to the gates. The corralled cattle backed away, bunching as far from the gate as they could get. He opened both gates. 'Line 'em up in the gate,' he instructed.

Realization began to dawn on the rustlers, and their faces turned ashen as though the same colour drain had been opened at each of their necklines.

'You ain't goin' to hang us, are you?' one gasped.

'Now or later, don't make much difference,' Levi gritted. He waved a gun barrel to his posse. 'Do it.'

The men led the outlaws' horses into the corral, turned them around near the milling, nervous cattle, and lined them up in a row in the gate.

'Throw some lariats over that top rail, and put the loops on 'em,' he ordered.

With much less reluctance than he had expected, the men hurried to do as he bid. In minutes the men were lined up neatly. A rope looped around each neck, then extended upward over the top gate brace, then down to where it was secured around a post. Their hands were all tied behind them. They were helpless.

Their horses were prancing nervously. They tried desperately to control them with their knees, knowing their lives were measured in minutes when the horses moved out from under them. A man moved forward to hold each horse's reins.

'Anyone got any last words?' Levi asked harshly.

One of the men was crying softly. 'Tell . . . tell my uncle I'm sorry,' he said. 'He . . . he tried to make me quit.'

'Who are you?' Levi responded.

'Toby. Tobias Olson. My . . . my . . . my uncle's Oscar Olson. He thought I was mixed up in this. He tried to tell me I was goin' to come to this. I kept tellin' him I wasn't. Just . . . just tell 'im I'm sorry.'

'Quitchyer blubberin' an' take your medicine,' one of the others growled.

'I don't suppose it would do any good to offer any kind of a deal, would it?' the youngest of the four asked.

Levi walked up close and looked at him. He was still in his teens. His Adam's apple bobbed up and down furiously. 'What kind of deal?' he asked.

'If we tell you who the one is behind it, will you take us to jail instead of hanging us?' the youngster asked hopefully.

'I'd consider it,' Levi acknowledged. 'If you name him quick and no games.'

'I'll tell you!' the young man said. 'It's . . .'

A shot rang out from behind the group. The young man's voice stopped in mid-word as a hole appeared between his eyes.

Levi and his men dove for cover. A second shot rang out, and young Olson grunted. Levi spotted the gunpowder flash from the corner of the depot, and fired four quick shots in return. Others had seen it as well, and wood flew from that corner of the building as a thunderous volley of shots sought the hidden sniper.

At the first shots, the men holding the rustlers' horses released them to dive for cover. The already nervous horses bolted. The two rustlers who had not been shot tried with frantic desperation to grip their horses tightly enough to control them with their knees. It served only to jerk them harder against the loops about their necks.

Two rustlers hung limply, already killed by the hidden marksman. The other two kicked out their lives at the ends of the ropes. Those who might at least have noted their dying were too busy preserving their own lives, too busy firing their guns at sounds and shadows, to even be aware. With life swirling all around them, their lives ebbed away in a private pool of loneliness.

The fighting lulled as the posse realized they were shooting at nothing. In the sudden silence that followed, Levi heard a horse pounding away at a dead run. Catching the flying reins of one of the rustler's horses, he lunged into the saddle and ran headlong, in pursuit.

He returned thirty minutes later. 'Lost 'im,' he lamented, in response to their questioning looks. 'Never even got a look at 'im.'

The group stood looking at the four rustlers, still swinging gently at the ends of their ropes. 'Did you really intend to hang them?' Homer asked softly.

Levi sighed heavily. 'Not for a minute,' he admitted. 'I just thought if they were sure we were going to, at least one of them would trade his neck for the name of the boss. I never thought of the boss already being here, hiding and waiting.'

'Gonna be hard on Lottie Olson,' Henry said softly.

'Going to be hard on several mothers,' Levi agreed sadly.

20

The macabre procession rode slowly through the streets of Chadron to the office of the Dawes County sheriff. By the time they arrived, nearly fifty people had joined the crowd following them. Levi rode in tight-lipped silence, but the others of the posse were not so reticent. They entered town in a sombre mood, but they began to realize almost at once that they were heroes. That realization changed them quickly to a holiday mood. They straightened in their saddles. They moved their guns to a more conspicuous position. They brushed at the dirt and dust that covered them. They shouted answers back to the questions yelled from the spectators. Their sombre entry changed into a victory procession for the adoration of the crowds.

Watching their response to the

accolades, Levi's lips tightened even more. The muscles at his temples bulged. He dismounted at the sheriff's office and walked inside without a word. The rest sat with the grisly display of corpses tied across their saddles. They answered questions. They held court before an admiring and growing crowd.

Levi walked into the sheriff's office and sat down wordlessly. The sheriff glared at him. 'I thought I told you I didn't want no turkey shoot.'

'We killed three of them, when we tried to arrest them,' Levi said.

The silence built until the sheriff dispelled it. 'I counted seven bodies comin' up the street.'

'The man we're lookin' for killed the others.'

The sheriff leaned back and glared at Levi. 'Well, maybe you'd best start at the beginning and tell me what happened.'

Levi told him the whole story. He offered no excuse for placing the four captives in a position that ultimately cost them their lives. 'I had no way to know he was hidin' there,' he offered. 'I had less idea that he'd kill his own men in cold blood, rather than let them tell who he was.'

The sheriff chewed on the information for quite a while. His face softened into a resignation filled with regret. 'He's a cold one, all right,' he mused. 'You got any ideas what to do next?'

'Yeah, I have an idea. There won't be any more rustling for a while, so we can back off on trying to watch cattle and catch them. I've got some riding to do.'

The sheriff waited for further explanation, but none was forthcoming. He shrugged. 'What about Olson? You still think he's the wrong man?'

Levi leaned back and stared at the ceiling thoughtfully. 'One of the rustlers is his nephew. That brings it pretty close to home. The boy said Oscar was tryin' to get him out of it. That means Oscar knew about it. He knew the boy was involved, but the boy said he told him he wasn't. I don't think he's the one we're lookin' for.'

'I don't see why not.'

'It just ain't the kind of operation a man with Oscar's disposition would run.'

'You could be wrong.'

'Wouldn't be the first time,' he said, with a pained look crossing his eyes. He sighed heavily and repeated the words. 'Wouldn't be the first time.'

'Well, I don't agree with you. I think my duty lies in arresting him, at least. I got to show the voters in this county I'm doing something to enforce the law.'

'Wouldn't hurt,' Levi agreed. 'I ain't sure I can keep Malone from organizing a lynch mob anyway. If you arrest Oscar, at least he'll be safe from that.'

'I'll deputize your posse to go after him.'

'I'll be askin' you to take the two bodies that belong out that way to their families, then, too,' Levi said.

'Two?'

He nodded. 'Young Olson. His folks are homesteaded along Bordeaux Creek. There's Bucky Conlon, too. His folks live . . . '

'I know where his family lives,' the sheriff growled. 'This is gonna bust his ma's heart. She's as fine a woman as ever lived in this country. Sure deserves better'n that lazy ne'er-do-well she married, I'll say that.'

Levi rose and started for the door. 'Hope you have better luck gettin' Oscar in here alive than I did the others,' he said. He left without waiting for a reply.

The crowd was bigger than ever when he went outside. He ignored a half-dozen questions shouted at him. He spoke to Henry. 'Henry, the sheriff will deputize the bunch of you and tell you what to do with the bodies. Then he wants you to ride with him out to Olson's. He'll be arrestin' Oscar.'

Henry looked at him sharply. 'You

change your mind?'

'I ain't sure,' he admitted. 'It looks bad for him, but my gut still says it ain't him. Anyway, he's better off in jail now, 'cause most of the country thinks he's it. Try to see to it he lives to get here.'

Henry nodded, looking over the group. 'I think I can trust all these men to use their heads,' he said. 'Once we get 'em outa town, that is.'

Still ignoring the crowd and its questions, Levi mounted his horse and rode out.

He rode south, riding hard and steady for two days. He left the pine ridge buttes and canyons, climbing to the table land that lay to its south. Beyond the table land he entered the rolling treeless hills and canyons of broken plains. He camped the first night along Cottonwood Creek. At first light he was in the saddle again.

At dark he was close enough to see scattered lights of the town of Alliance. That night he put his horse in a livery barn, and spent the night at a hotel. They both needed the rest.

The next day he waited for the bank to open. When it did, he asked to see the president. He identified himself, then asked his question.

'I need to know whether one of the ranchers, or anyone else for that matter, from over the other side of Pepper Creek has an account here.'

'I can't tell you that.'

'Well sir, it'd save some trouble if you could. There's a need to find out where the money from the rustlin' is goin'. Chances are, the boss of that outfit ain't keepin' it buried in a fruit jar someplace. Not with the kind o' men he's dealin' with.'

'I still can't tell you that. I have an obligation to my customers, you understand. I can't just go telling their business to anyone that walks in and identifies himself as some sort of investigator.'

'I am a deputy sheriff.'

'Not in this county, you're not.'

Levi considered the matter. Wordlessly he got up and walked out. He was back thirty minutes later with the Box Butte county sheriff. 'Earl,' the sheriff said without ceremony, 'this man is a legitimate law officer, on a legitimate mission. I want you to tell him whatever he needs to know. If I have to, I can get a court order from Judge Williamson to that effect.'

The banker looked annoyed. 'That will not be necessary. You understand, however, I'm only protecting my customers. I do have to have some legal authority to divulge that kind of information.'

'How about those accounts,' Levi insisted abruptly.

'Well the fact is,' the banker said, leaning back in his chair, 'we do not have a single account in this bank belonging to anyone living north of Pepper Creek.'

Levi felt a rising tide of rage. 'If you didn't have any, why'd you make me go get the sheriff before you told me that?' he asked.

He had walked around the man's desk, and was glowering down at him as he asked. The banker was unperturbed. He tipped his chair back on to its back legs and looked up at Levi archly. 'It's just a matter of principle.'

'Well, so's this,' Levi responded, kicking the legs out from under the chair.

The banker howled as he and the chair landed in a sudden heap on the floor. Levi winked at the sheriff and walked out. He could hear the pompous banker blustering and sputtering as he walked out the front door.

He did nothing more that day, reasoning that his horse needed a day's rest. He was in the saddle when the sun came up to look for him the following morning. It found him heading north, and quickly attached his shadow to him again. He swung a wide circle, seeking out every town around he thought likely for such an account. He found nothing.

It was almost two weeks later when he entered the sheriff's office in Chadron. 'It's time you showed up,' the sheriff groused. 'I've been getting all kinds of heat to either charge Olson with the rustling or find out who it is. What have you found?'

Levi told him what he had been searching for and his singular lack of success.

'What towns have you tried?' the sheriff asked finally.

Levi rattled off the list of cow towns and railroad towns he had checked over the past two weeks. 'Just about covered all of them,' the sheriff agreed. 'Can't think anyone would ride further than you been. It's got to be some place he can ride in a day. You try Wayside?'

'Wayside? Never heard of it.'

'Ain't too much of a town. Got a bank, though. It's north from Dakota Junction, just before the railroad goes over into Dakota. Might be worth a try.'

Levi rode out again the next morning. It was the next afternoon when he rode into Wayside. He rode directly to the bank. It was closed, but he could see activity inside. He pounded on the door.

After he had pounded intermittently for nearly five minutes, a face finally appeared in the glass. 'We're closed up,' the face said.

Levi held up his badge. 'I need to talk to you,' he said.

The face peered at him indecisively for a long moment, then the lock rattled in the door. It swung open only slightly. 'Can't it wait till we're open?'

'Sorry to push it,' Levi said. 'I'd rather not be around when you open up tomorrow. I need to ask you some questions.'

The man looked him over carefully, then sighed. 'Well, come on in so I can lock the door again.'

When they were seated, Levi spelled out the situation and told him what he was asking for. The banker went into the vault and emerged with several large ledgers. He put them on his desk and began to pore over them.

'We have several customers from that general area,' he said, 'but only a couple from south of Chadron. Ah, here's the one I had noticed. This person has made a rather large number of substantial deposits, but no withdrawals at all. All his deposits have been in cash, which is not too unusual, but I have wondered at the amount of those deposits.'

'Can you give me the amounts and dates?'

'Very well,' the banker nodded, and began to recount a series of deposits dating back well over a year. Levi compared the dates with a list the sheriff had supplied him. It was a list of dates when bunches of cattle were known to have disappeared. The dates bore a rough correspondence that could not have been coincidence.

'Pay dirt!' Levi said softly.

'I beg your pardon?' the banker said, looking at Levi across the top of his glasses.

'Pay dirt!' Levi repeated. 'Go back down that list of dates and I'll read you a list of dates when cattle are known to have been stolen.'

As he read his list of dates, the banker kept bobbing his head until Levi thought he looked like a woodpecker. The last deposit was one day after Levi had watched the cattle buyer pay the mastermind of the rustlers.

'I guess I'll have to ask you for his name,' he said.

The banker hesitated only for a moment. 'I'm not sure it is entirely legal without a court order,' he said, 'but under the circumstances that would only be a matter of you wasting two more days in the saddle to procure that and return. I see no reason, in as much as you are a duly authorized officer of the law, that I cannot give that name to you: it is Walter Hebert.'

Levi's jaw dropped. He felt as if

he had been struck in the stomach. A hundred thoughts fluttered through his mind and not one of them would settle enough for him to grasp hold of it. He knew he was sitting like a slack-jawed dolt, but he just could not move.

'Is something wrong?' the banker asked.

'I . . . uh . . . I . . . uh, no,' he said weakly, as his mind watched the fledgling shoots of a new dream wither and die. 'No. It's just that I thought I knew who it was. Walt's name never occurred to me. It . . . uh . . . it fits. Uh . . . OK. Well, thanks. I'm much obliged.'

He got up to leave. At the door he stopped and returned. 'I'll be needin' a list of the dates and amounts of those deposits.'

'Certainly,' the banker complied. 'I assume this means we will be losing Mr Hebert as a customer.'

'I reckon,' Levi said sadly. 'That money'll have to go back to the folks he stole the cows from. What's left of it, at least.'

'I will hold the account until the matter is settled. I would appreciate any good word you could put in for this bank with those folks,' the banker said, as he worked on writing the list.

Levi did not answer. He accepted the list and left.

21

Levi sat in the sheriff's office. He had left Wayside only the day before. The ride to Chadron had seemed interminable. His jaw was set. A hollow emptiness seemed to reach out from the caverns of his eyes.

'Well I'll be danged!' the sheriff breathed. 'I've always been impressed with the kind of place Walt could maintain with the amount of land he has, but I sure never thought of him as a thief. This'll go hard on his family.'

Levi nodded. His mind was filled with thoughts of one member of that family in particular. 'He's a cool customer. He's always came out pretty strong in my defence whenever Oscar tried to make folks think I was involved. He's one that ageed to bring me here to start with. I reckon he did it to keep any suspicion from himself.

It sure worked. I never in my wildest dreams thought it was him.'

'Well, I think we have ample evidence to arrest him now,' the sheriff opined.

Levi disagreed. 'All we got right now is a list of dates when he put money in the bank. All he's got to do is come up with some reason he got that money just then. With the money he paid the ones doing the rustling, and the money he spent on his own place, the amounts ain't going to tally with the cattle stolen.'

The sheriff considered the matter. 'It's enough evidence to arrest the man,' he argued. 'I owe it to the voters to do that. What the court does with it is the judge's responsibility. There's also the matter of a large amount of the money recovered from the belongings of the dead rustlers.'

'I'd like to sew it up tighter,' Levi said. 'Give me a couple days.'

'What are you up to now?' the sheriff asked suspiciously.

'Just an idea. Would you put out the

word that the Cattlemen's Association will meet at Bertram's again day after tomorrow?'

The sheriff hesitated a while, then shrugged. 'It's your party. You want me there?'

'I reckon.'

The sheriff nodded and Levi left.

Levi was purposely late for the meeting. He wanted to be sure everyone was present ahead of him. When he entered Bertram's yard, the entire membership of the Association was inside.

He crossed behind the tethered horses until he came to Walt Hebert's horse. He opened the saddlebags and reached in. He withdrew a pair of boots. He turned them over, looking at the soles. Then he put his hands in them and pressed them into the dust of the yard. He stood looking at the footprints. 'Pay dirt!' he whispered.

He stepped up and walked across the porch loudly, entering the house without knocking. The buzz of conversation stopped. He crossed to the far end of the room where the sheriff was sitting, and wheeled to face the assembled group. He began without preamble.

'I asked you to meet here to wrap up the matter of the rustling I was brought here to solve. At Dakota Junction, we surrounded and captured the entire crew that were actually doing the driving of the cattle. Three of them were shot before the rest surrendered. The other four were made ready for hanging. I did not intend to hang them, but to force them to name the man who was behind the whole thing.

'To a degree, I reckon it worked. Two of them agreed at once to give us that name in exchange for being arrested instead of hanged. Before they could tell us the name, they were shot from ambush. In the hubbub, the horses ran out from under the other two and they hanged.

'I did talk to one of the three who was shot, though, before he died.'

That statement caused a sudden stir

of conversation, but he held up his hand for silence and continued, 'On the basis of what that man told me, I've spent the past couple of weeks riding to other towns to find out if the man who is the brains behind this rustling had a bank account somewhere he was salting away the money.'

A murmur of excitement and appreciation rippled around the room, and he again held up his hand for silence. 'I found it.'

This time, instead of noise, the announcement was met with a breathless silence.

'I'd like to read you a list of dates and deposits in that account. You can match them with the dates when you know cattle was stolen.'

He read the list, watching the growing air of excitement as he did so. When he finished, he continued to speak into the expectant stillness. 'I knew for a long time it had to be someone in the Association. They never went after a herd that was guarded and they knew every move we were making. Like the rest of you, I was pretty sure it was Oscar Olson: it wasn't.'

A sudden explosion of jabbering forced him to wait for silence again. 'Oscar did know something and he didn't want me here to investigate. He had a nephew, as you all know by now, that he thought was involved in it. He was. Oscar thought if he could keep them from getting caught long enough, he could catch the kid, or make him admit he was in it and force him out. He just didn't want him getting killed or sent to prison.'

'What about all that money he used to pay off his place?' Casey Malone demanded.

'It came from his wife's uncle,' Levi explained. 'I talked to the Hay Springs banker about it myself. He wouldn't admit where it came from because he didn't want anybody knowin' he was ridin' on his wife's skirt tails to pay his bills.'

He looked all around the room,

carefully avoiding making any direct eye contact with Walt Hebert, but very much aware of his presence. He went on, 'The one thing that really threw me was the tracks. I'm a tracker. I'm a right good tracker. I can track a grasshopper across a flat rock by moonlight. I knew if I ever saw the tracks of the man who shot Robert, I'd know them. I saw those same tracks where he met the rustlers at Dakota Junction. I had never seen those tracks anywhere else — until today.'

He waited for the excited buzz to die down again. 'I saw them today because I found the boots that made them. They were in the man's saddle-bags, instead of on his feet.

'The name on the bank account is the same as the owner of the horse where I found those boots. It's the same name the dying rustler gave me. I've checked it out and I have absolute proof the one behind this rustling is Walt Hebert.'

As he said the man's name, Levi

pointed at the rancher. A gasp of disbelief escaped twenty some throats at once. Before anyone but Levi even realized it, Walt Hebert had a .45 in each hand.

'You're good, Hill,' the rancher said calmly.

As all eyes turned to him everyone realized suddenly that gunfire was imminent. There was a surge of bodies away from the area between Levi and Walt. In the matter of a single breath Levi was at one end of the room and Walt was at the other, with nobody between.

'It's no good, Walt,' Levi said calmly. 'There's too many guns here for you to be able to walk out.'

'Oh, you could probably kill me,' Walt conceded, 'but there's a lot of you going to die if you try.'

'Why'd you do it, Walt?' Chet Buchanan asked, the pain of a friend's betrayal heavy in his voice.

Walt gave a short hard laugh. 'Money, Chet. Money. I like a nice place. My family deserves a nice place. I like to buy strange animals that nobody else's got. I just didn't have land enough or cattle enough to provide it. It was the easiest thing in the world to let you fellows help me have it. Now clear a way to the door! I'm walking out of here, and I'll kill anyone who gets in my way.'

A .45 boomed incredibly loud in the enclosed room. Walt jerked backward a step and looked at his shirt front with an uncomprehending stare. He looked back at the smoking gun nobody had seen appear in Levi's hand. He brought his right-hand gun up slightly, but was jarred by another bullet from Levi's gun slamming into him. He frowned in confusion.

'How'd you . . . how'd you . . . '

Both guns slipped from his grasp and clattered on to the floor. He fell forward on to them and lay without moving.

There was a long moment of total silence. It was the sheriff who broke it. 'You cut that mighty close, Hill.'

Levi shrugged. 'I had to get him to confess. That seemed like the easiest way. Sheriff, I'd take it kindly if you'd ask the judge to go easy on Olson.'

He turned to Henry. 'Henry, I thank you for all the help. You've been a friend.'

'You leavin'?' Henry asked. 'Just like that?'

Levi nodded. 'Job's done. Pinkerton'll deal with the Association for what they owe. I'll be stoppin' by your place to pick up my stuff.'

With only a glance around, he strode to the door and went outside. As he mounted his horse the sheriff came out.

'Hill, I owe you. I'm much obliged. If you'd be interested, I could sure use you on a permanent basis.'

Levi shook his head. 'I'm headin' back to Wyoming,' he said. 'This is a good country. Good folks mostly. But I reckon it's seen about all o' me it can stand just now.'

'It ain't going to go easy on Naomi,' the sheriff said pointedly. 'A woman don't deserve to lose two men in one day.'

Levi stared hard at the sheriff for a long moment. The muscles along his jaw knotted and loosened rhythmically. Finally he said, 'Sheriff, that man I just killed was her pa. If there was anything between us or ever could have been, I just killed it.'

The sheriff nodded reluctantly. 'Well, if you ever change your mind and want to come back to this country, I'll have a job for you or I'll find one for you. This country can use men like you.'

Levi nodded wordlessly. Lifting the reins, he turned the horse and trotted from the yard. If he had looked back he would have seen the entire Cattlemen's Association watching him ride away. He didn't look back.

Other titles in the Linford Western Library

THE CROOKED SHERIFF
John Dyson

Black Pete Bowen quit Texas with a burning hatred of men who try to take the law into their own hands. But he discovers that things aren't much different in the silver mountains of Arizona.

THEY'LL HANG BILLY FOR SURE:
Larry & Stretch
Marshall Grover

Billy Reese, the West's most notorious desperado, was to stand trial. From all compass points came the curious and the greedy, the riff-raff of the frontier. Suddenly, a crazed killer was on the loose — but the Texas Trouble-Shooters were there, girding their loins for action.

RIDERS OF RIFLE RANGE
Wade Hamilton

Veterinarian Jeff Jones did not like open warfare — but it was there on Scrub Pine grass. When he diagnosed a sick bull on the Endicott ranch as having the contagious blackleg disease, he got involved in the warfare — whether he liked it or not!

BEAR PAW
Nevada Carter

Austin Dailey traded two cows to a pair of Indians for a bay horse, which subsequently disappeared. Tracks led to a secret hideout of fugitive Indians — and cattle thieves. Indians and stockmen co-operated against the rustlers. But it was Pale Woman who acted as interpreter between her people and the rangemen.

THE WEST WITCH
Lance Howard

Detective Quinton Hilcrest journeys west, seeking the Black Hood Bandits' lost fortune. Within hours of arriving in Hags Bend, he is fighting for his life, ensnared with a beautiful outcast the town claims is a witch! Can he save the young woman from the angry mob?

GUNS OF THE PONY EXPRESS
T. M. Dolan

Rich Zennor joined the Pony Express venture at the start, as second-in-command to tough Denning Hartman. But Zennor had the problems of Hartman believing that they had crossed trails in the past, and the fact that he was strongly attached to Hartman's Indian girl, Conchita.

BLACK JO OF THE PECOS
Jeff Blaine

Nobody knew where Black Josephine Callard came from or whither she returned. Deputy U.S. Marshal Frank Haggard would have to exercise all his cunning and ability to stay alive before he could defeat her highly successful gang and solve the mystery.

RIDE FOR YOUR LIFE
Johnny Mack Bride

They rode west, hoping for a new start. Then they met another broken-down casualty of war, and he had a plan that might deliver them from despair. But the only men who would attempt it would be the truly brave — or the desperate. They were both.